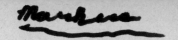

SCOTTY
and the MYSTERIOUS
MESSAGE

By

BETTY SWINFORD

MOODY PRESS
CHICAGO

Printed in the United States of America

SCOTTY
and the MYSTERIOUS
MESSAGE

CONTENTS

Chapter One

STRANGE MESSAGE

THE GREAT WHITE HORSE left brown flurries of dust behind his hoofs. He'd thundered along for two miles, silken mane flowing. And still he wanted to gallop, until Scotty was forced to rein his horse to a walk.

"You'll have other times to run, Rocky. No sense running yourself to death all in one day. Besides," he grinned, "poor little Butch is back there about ready to drop!"

Danny, riding alongside Scotty, laughed out loud. "He sure is! His tongue is hanging out, and his legs are about to collapse under him."

The boys stopped their mounts until the little black and white bulldog caught up. But Butch was grinning broadly and, like a good sport, was wagging his tail vigorously. Once caught up to the fellows, however, he plopped down right on the worn cattle trail and panted with all his might.

"You'll be OK, Butch," Scotty encouraged. "Just

7

a little more and we'll be back home again. Come
on, fellow!"

"I heard your Aunt Margaret is coming to visit,"
Danny murmured after a minute.

Scotty's freckles dipped down into a quick little
frown, but he pretended that it was from holding
Rocky in so tight. "Aunt Margaret's coming tonight, but she'll only be with us overnight."

"Don't you like her?"

Scotty's dark eyes whipped to his friend's face.
"Oh sure, Danny. Aunt Margaret's all right. She's
just old and sort of boring to Susan and me, that's
all. I dread having to sit around all evening talking. It's lots more fun to read in my room or play
checkers with Susan or something."

"Yeah." Danny pushed his western hat back and
wiped the little beads of sweat from his forehead.
"I don't have any aunts, so I guess I wouldn't understand. Honest, I don't see why we have to sit
in with grown-ups. Like family reunions— I used
to *hate* family reunions. No guys my age, and
what fellows there were, acted like they were just
years and years older than me. It was *awful!*"

Scotty smiled in sympathy. "Let's stop at the
reservoir for a drink, OK? I feel like I've got a
wad of cotton in my mouth."

The boys brought their mounts close so they
could drink from the cold, clear water. Scotty
found a coffee can and filled it for Butch. Then he

put his face in the water where the pipe sent it gushing forth, fresh and clean, and drank deeply. He was studying his face on the water and watching it reflect the snowy-white thunderheads against the blue, blue sky when Susan came riding up the trail.

Spotting her brother, she urged her horse into a gallop.

Scotty looked up, pressing his sleeve against his wet lips. "Oh-oh."

"Sisters!" Danny growled. "Wonder what she wants with you?"

Susan reined her horse to a stop but did not dismount. "Guess what, Scotty?" There wasn't very much joy in her voice.

"What's up?" Scotty twisted his mouth to one side and waited.

Susan sighed. "Aunt Margaret came early, and she wants to see you. In her words, 'I just can't wait to see my little nephew again.'"

Scotty sighed. "Oh boy !" He told himself that he was a Christian, and that as a follower of the Lord Jesus Christ he must treat his aunt with deep respect. This helped a lot, but it did not totally erase his own private feelings.

"This is where I bow out!" Danny grunted. "See you tomorrow afternoon, Scot." He grinned. "If anything exciting happens, call me."

Danny leaped into the saddle and was gone in

a cloud of dust. Looking after him, Scotty murmured softly, "I could envy him."

"Oh, come on, Scot! You know Aunt Margaret's not that bad."

Scotty swung onto Rocky's back and scooped Butch up under one arm. "I know, Susan. It's just the way she pinches my cheek and talks like I'm a two-year-old. Why can't she see that we're growing up?"

"We'll survive her visit," Susan said firmly. "I know it's dull and all that, but this time, Scotty, we're Christians—remember? Let's do our very best, not for Aunt Margaret, but for Jesus. OK, Scotty?"

Scotty thought for a moment. A feeling of shame came stealing through his most secret heart. Finally he gave Susan his best smile. "Yes. I can do it for Jesus, Susan."

Yes. Sure he could. No trick to that at all. Scotty would be polite and kind and all the rest. She'd see Christ in his life and perhaps she too would be drawn to the Saviour.

The house at the Diamond W Ranch came into sight. Scotty always thrilled when he started down the trail toward the ranch from this point, for the whole ranch could be seen, nestled in the little valley. The one-story, rambling house with its pink tiled roof and its trailing green ivy, the big cottonwood tree in the yard and the orange trees, bright with golden fruit, the bunkhouse near the arroyo, the corrals where horses neighed impatiently, the big hay barn and other smaller buildings. Around all this were the rolling foothills, covered with cactus and mesquite and dotted with red and white Hereford steers.

The two young people dismounted slowly and turned their horses into the corral. And now for Aunt Margaret!

Scotty tried to hold his head high and his shoulders square as he marched inside the house. He said, "Hi, Mom," to his mother and wondered how someone so sweet and so pretty ever managed to have a sister like Aunt Margaret.

There she was—flitting around the room like a hummingbird and twittering more like a canary. Seeing Scotty, she pounced on him like an eagle snatching up its prey—at least to Scotty's mind. Aunt Margaret kissed him soundly, hugged him hard, and smacked the seat of his jeans as one might pat a baby in three-cornered pants. It was almost more than Scotty could bear.

"Hi, Aunt Margaret," he managed feebly.

"Scotty! Why, I do believe my little man is beginning to grow up. I just can't believe how tall you are," she said, wagging her head, her red-dyed hair flouncing.

"I'm twelve," he said grimly.

She fussed over him and Susan all through supper, and finally, when the Hanson family had gathered in the living room for the evening, Aunt Margaret brought out presents. She always brought Scotty and his sister presents, though they usually turned out to be for children much younger. With this in mind, they smiled, steeled themselves, and tried desperately to act normal.

Aunt Margaret gave Scotty his package first. It was all done in red and gold paper, but it had pictures on it of boys about five years old. He accepted the package with a smile and waited until Susan had her present too.

"Go ahead, Scot," Susan urged. "Open yours first."

He gave her a look that said what his lips did not dare say and tore open the paper. A moment later he swallowed painfully. He'd suspected it would be something to embarrass him. But *a little toy train?* That was almost too much. He hadn't played with little trains like this since he was six.

"Thanks!" he choked. "Thanks a lot, Aunt Margaret!"

"Oh, you sweet boy!" She pinched his cheek with her plump, ringed hand and chattered away. If Scotty hadn't caught his mother's understanding smile, he couldn't have stood it.

Susan, realizing that her aunt was waiting and that she wouldn't be satisfied until she opened her present, began ever so slowly to unwrap her gift.

A moment later she found herself holding a golden-haired talking doll, the kind Susan had received for Christmas when she was ten. Scotty saw the look on her face and felt sorry for her.

"Th-thanks, Aunt Margaret. She's beautiful, and she's wearing a lovely red velvet dress." Susan swallowed. "I think she'll look neat sitting on my vanity."

Somehow during the next half hour Scotty and his sister managed to escape to their rooms. Scotty closed his door and stood against it for a moment, almost fearing lest Aunt Margaret follow him. He smoothed back his dark hair with a loud sigh.

"Well, that's over. Almost, at least!" He put the train, still in its box, on his cedar chest and went to his long glass door to stare outside into the moonlight. "We'll take her to Tucson in the morning and put her on the train, and that'll be that." He sighed again. "Boy, I'm glad I'm not blessed with four or five aunts like her."

He showered and put his pajamas on. Too tired to read his Bible or pray tonight! He was just going. . . .

Now wait a minute!

Scotty's head shot up. Boy, that was almost like a real voice. His conscience was really on the ball. He pressed his lips together firmly.

"Sly old boy, the devil!" he murmured half aloud. "Dad and Mom aren't leading in family devotions

tonight, so right away I'm tempted to slide into
bed and forget God. Well, I'm not going to do
any such thing!"

With new determination, Scotty picked up his
Bible and read from the book of John. He loved
Philippians and Colossians, especially Colossians
1:18 where it said, "That in all things He might
have the preeminence." But somehow he loved
John best of all.

Scotty was just getting up from his knees when
there came a soft rap at his door. He jumped.
Aunt Margaret! Probably coming to kiss him goodnight. He thought he'd die if—

He opened his door just a slit and drooped with
relief when he saw that it was only Susan. She
came inside quickly and closed the door behind
her. On second thought, she turned and locked it.

"What's the matter with you?" Scotty grinned.
"Playing with your doll and don't want anyone to
see you?"

Susan pursed her lips and gave a toss of her
blond hair. She drew back as though to throw the
doll at Scotty, and he ducked around to the other
side of the bed.

Laughing, Scotty stood with his hands on his
hips. "OK, sis, you go ahead and play dolls. But
just don't come into my bedroom wanting me to
play with you, because I won't."

Susan had fire in her blue eyes as she turned to

march out of Scotty's room. "OK, smarty, if you don't want to hear about the mystery, I'll just share it with someone else."

She opened the door and started to leave, but Scotty leaped over his bed and pulled at her arm. "Wait a minute, Sue! What are you talking about?"

She made a face at him. "I thought that would bring you to your senses. And, if I decide to tell you, don't you dare accuse me of playing dolls. I was just about to put her on my vanity, and I decided that, just for fun, I'd pull the string in her back to see what she said. Here," she went on, thrusting the doll into Scotty's hands, "see what I mean!"

Twisting his mouth to one side and heaving a long sigh, Scotty gave the string a pull. The words came out distinctly.

> A ranch, a cave, a stone;
> They're one and yet they're three.
> From two and down the river,
> Four paces left to the chinaberry tree.

Scotty scratched his ear. Butch cocked his head and whined at this strange message. The boy played it again.

"Whoever heard tell of a man's voice talking through a doll?" Susan cried softly.

"Whoever heard tell of reciting a crazy poem

like that?" Scott added. "It doesn't make any sense at all."

They stood looking at one another for a long time. Was this someone's idea of a joke? Scotty had a strange feeling that it wasn't. Somehow, in some way, there was a deep mystery connected with this doll.

Chapter Two

MR. KARL SHOPS FOR DOLLS

THE ROOM IN WHICH SCOTTY and his sister stood was filled with silence. Scotty stood in his pajamas with feet wide apart and a look of unbelief stamped upon his freckled face. Susan stood with the doll in her hands, her finger hanging limply in the hook on the end of the string that set the talking box to going. Butch sat looking up at the scene with a big question mark in his brown eyes. The sound that finally broke the stillness was the *thump-thump* of the dog's tail against the bare floor.

Scotty knelt beside his black and white bulldog and stroked the velvet ears. "You're wondering about things too, aren't you, fellow? Sure is strange, putting a man's voice saying a crazy poem in a doll."

Finally Susan gave a shrug of her shoulders. "Oh well, maybe the man in the doll factory was putting in the talking boxes and just got carried away with the idea of a silly joke."

Scotty frowned first, then nodded. "Sure. That's got to be the answer. What else *could* it be, anyway?"

Susan forced herself to laugh. "I don't really think it was a very funny joke. Suppose some little girl had received this doll for her birthday. Or maybe a child who was sick and in the hospital."

"That's right," Scotty agreed. "At least we can be thankful that the doll was given to you instead of to a little girl! What are you going to do, let Aunt Margaret exchange it or just keep it?"

Susan touched the bright red velvet dress. "I'll just keep it. After all, I won't be listening to it talk. It'll just be to look at, so it won't matter. We won't say anything about it."

As Susan slipped from his room, Scotty turned back to the window. He loved the nights at the Diamond W. The sky was like black velvet and the stars hung against it like dazzling jewels that changed in color from blue to red to white. Truly the heavens showed the glory of God!

Sleep was hard to find that night, and Scotty's dreams were filled with a doll that talked with a man's voice and said things that didn't make sense.

> A ranch, a cave, a stone;
> They're one and yet they're three.
> From two and down the river,
> Four paces left to the chinaberry tree.

Scotty sat bolt upright in bed and Butch, sleeping on the foot of the bed, moved close and licked his master's hand.

Scotty frowned and sighed deeply. "That silly poem again. Boy!"

He lay back slowly, listening to the lonely cry of a coyote up in the hills. A moment later there was an answering cry. It was a sound that never failed to stir Scotty's heart, for it was a cry as lonely as his own heart's cry had been before he had found Jesus as his Saviour. What a wonderful day not too long ago when he had discovered that the blood of Jesus could wash away every sin and bring joy and peace to his heart.

Before sleep claimed him again, pale gray and pink streaks began to show up in the sky east of the ranch. Daylight was on the way.

No sense going back to bed. He couldn't sleep anyway. Scotty slipped into his jeans, scuffed black boots, and blue checkered shirt and stepped out his door. He'd just take a walk down to the corral and see Rocky until his folks got up. After— *What was that?*

Butch lowered his stocky little body to the ground and the hair along his spine rose to stiff peaks. A low growl escaped his throat. Scotty scooped up the animal and stepped into the long shadow of a pepper tree. There was a man walking through the hills away behind the corral!

Scotty continued to watch him until he was out of sight. Then the boy slowly relaxed. Just a hunter, no doubt. But he shouldn't be hunting on the ranch property. A hunter could just as easily kill a steer when shooting at deer. Besides, it wasn't deer season, and Scotty was sure it was a rifle the man had been carrying. Oh well, maybe he was hunting cottontails and it was a shotgun instead. No sense building up another mystery in his imagination. The doll had done enough of that!

Butch let out a few short yelps even after Scotty put him down. Then, feeling that he had done his duty, he went on with his master to the corral.

Rocky came to the split rail fence, tossing his powerful white head up and down and neighing in welcome. Scotty remembered the trouble he'd had raising this horse and how everyone had thought Rocky was loco. Except for many answers to prayer, Rocky probably would have ended up in the glue factory a long time ago.

"You're a great horse, Rocky. The best there is! I don't know what I'd do without you."

Rocky lipped Scotty's ear as if to say he was feeling the same way. They understood each other well, those two. They both loved the hard rides across the hills, the quiet moonlight walks when they depended on the horse's eyes to take them safely, and they loved the times when they camped overnight with Danny or with Mr. Hanson. It would be very hard to get along without Rocky.

"Son!"

Scotty turned around from where he sat atop the fence and saw his father standing in the doorway of Scotty's bedroom.

"What is it, Dad?"

"We just checked on your Aunt Margaret's train, and it leaves earlier than we thought. Come in for breakfast so we can get going."

"Sure, Dad!"

Scotty gave Rocky's neck a final pat, then slid to the ground. Well, well, well! How good could things get, anyhow? Good old Aunt Margaret was on her way early. No more kisses, pats, or smacks.

He choked down the bacon and eggs in record time and was a little bit ashamed of himself for eating so fast just to get away from his aunt.

To ride into Tucson in the station wagon took twenty-five minutes. When Susan and Scotty were given permission to go window shopping while their parents saw Aunt Margaret off, Scotty felt like leaping for joy.

"Good-bye, Scotty dear!" Aunt Margaret cooed. "Be a good little boy for Mother, won't you? Aunt Margaret will see you again next year."

Scotty saw two fellows about his age listening and then ducking their heads and rolling back and forth in laughter. He wanted to die right on the spot!

"Good-bye, Aunt Margaret." And he managed to twist out from under her arm before she could land a kiss on his cheek. "Come on, Susan!"

Scotty dug his fists deeply into his pockets and walked along, silently pondering. "She's not like Mom," he managed at last.

"Hardly," was all Susan had to say.

Downtown stores were just opening for the day, and streets were bustling with people. Scotty and Susan were wandering aimlessly down Congress Street when Scotty suddenly paused before a store window.

"Hey, Sue, come take a look. There are some dolls in the window just like the one Aunt Margaret got for you. She must have stopped here after she got off the train."

Susan backtracked two or three steps. "A toy store! And the dolls *do* look like the one I have, except that these have on blue dresses instead of red ones." Susan bit her lip and her blue eyes said that she was doing some deep thinking. "Scotty? Just for fun let's go inside and pull a string or two on these dolls to see what they say."

Scotty pursed his lips and nodded. "Yes sir, let's just do that." He grinned as they stepped inside. "Only I sure hope nobody walks by that knows me!"

As they walked inside the toy store, neither of them saw the short, muscular man with the thin lips and piercing blue eyes that was coming up the sidewalk.

"Over here by the window," Susan whispered.

"Good morning, young lady," said a voice from behind the counter. "May I help you?"

Scotty hesitated. "We're just looking," Susan smiled.

She picked up the doll near the window and pulled the string. It spoke immediately. "Will you play house with me?"

At that same moment the short, stocky man swung into the store, going directly to the counter where the other man stood.

"Good morning, Mr. Karl." And if Scotty had been looking, he would have noticed a strange new light in the eyes of the salesman.

"Sam! Good to see you. Say, my niece is coming for a visit, and I wanted to buy a present for her. Maybe a talking doll like the one that girl is looking at?"

Scotty nudged his sister. "Ready to go, Sue?"

"In a minute." She pulled the doll's string again and they listened.

"Will you kiss me goodnight?"

Scotty's face twisted. "For Pete's sake, sis, we've got our answer. Let's get out of here!"

"The dolls look fine," Mr. Karl was saying. "Just the thing I had in mind! Only I'm fond of red. Don't you have one dressed in red velvet?"

Scotty's hand on his sister's arm suddenly tensed. Susan pretended to be studying the doll very closely. They waited.

"As a matter of fact," Sam replied, "I believe one red-dressed doll did come in that last shipment. It's right under the counter here, all boxed and—" The man stooped for the box, and his mouth dropped open. A moment later he was down on his knees, his hands exploring the shelf feverishly.

"Is something wrong?" Mr. Karl asked.

"Yes! *No!* I don't know!" Sweat stood out on Sam's white face. He looked as if he was trembling. "It has to be here, Mr. Karl! It couldn't—" Suddenly his whole face sagged and he got limply to his feet. "Yesterday— I was off yesterday! But there was a SOLD tag on the box." He was speaking in a hushed whisper, but Scotty and Susan overheard.

Mr. Karl turned to look at the young people and Scotty passed slowly out of the store, his brown eyes still looking into the store window. Susan followed at his heels. But once outside the store, they both paused.

"You fool!" Mr. Karl hissed. "Do you realize what is going to happen if you don't find that doll for me?"

Chapter Three

MYSTERY CALLER

STANDING IN THE MORNING SHADOW just outside the doorway of the toy store, Scotty and his sister strained their ears to catch what Mr. Karl was saying.

"Look," Sam's voice trembled out, "I'll call the salesman who worked in the store yesterday. We'll find out—"

"You'd *better* find out!" Mr. Karl ground out bitterly. "The other two are worthless without this one. You find out by this afternoon, because *I'll be back!*"

Seconds later, before Scotty or Susan could move, Mr. Karl strode angrily from the store. His face was purple with rage. He passed the two without even seeing them.

"Well," Susan sighed. "What do you think about *this?*"

Scotty raised his eyebrows. "I think the dolls only come in blue and pink and that the red one was something extra special. I think somebody really goofed up a sale and—" He broke off and grinned. "I think we'd better get back to the train station."

They returned to Toole Avenue and crossed over to the train depot. Each was pondering this strange turn of events when suddenly Scotty stopped dead still. A frown sat upon his face as he pointed a brown finger toward three people standing in front of the depot.

"Oh no!" he groaned. "Aunt Margaret is still here. Her train must be late or something."

Susan lowered her voice. "Now listen to me, Scotty Hanson! No matter what the reason is that she's not gone yet, you be nice to her. She's old and kind of rickety, and she doesn't mean any harm. Do you hear me?"

"I hear you," Scotty muttered through clenched teeth. "But remember, you're a girl, and it's easier for you!"

He put on a smile as they neared his folks. "We're back, Dad. What's up?"

His mother answered. "There was a flash flood between here and Phoenix, and all the trains have been detained. Your Aunt Margaret decided to just stay over for a couple of weeks, so we put through a call to her daughter not to worry. We've been waiting for you so we can go home."

Scotty frowned, then pulled his face into grim lines and finally let it relax into a sick kind of smile. "Imagine that," he whispered.

Aunt Margaret put her arm around Scotty's shoulders and jabbered all the way to the car about what a lucky person she was to have such a sweet nephew and such a darling niece. Scotty braced himself and walked woodenly beside her. Boy, she fouled everything up. Even toy stores!

The Diamond W Ranch never looked better than it did today. By the time the family reached home, Scotty's stomach was rocking, and he wondered seriously if Aunt Margaret ever closed her mouth long enough to let anyone else talk. Susan had smiled and tried to be nice, but now even she was 'ooking a little green.

After lunch Susan retreated to her room with a book, locking the door behind her.

Scotty cleaned his room and went to the corral. He ran fresh water for the horses and gave them a little grain. Then he went into the tack room for Rocky's saddle and bridle. If ever he needed a good hard ride, it was surely this afternoon!

Butch waited by the water tank, whining anxiously.

"She's even bugged you, hasn't she, Butch?" Scotty asked bitterly.

He slung the saddle over the corral fence while he gave Rocky a quick brushdown. When he took the brush back into the tack room, his eyes fell upon a little dust-covered book lying on a narrow shelf. It was a New Testament he'd placed there

weeks before when he'd promised God to take a
few minutes out each morning for Bible reading
and prayer. He bit his lip as the Holy Spirit reminded him that he had not kept that promise.

Hesitantly he picked up the little book and
opened it. The words seemed to leap out at him.
The leper had come to Jesus, saying, "If thou wilt,
thou canst make me clean." And Jesus reached out
and *touched* the leper, a man who was no doubt
covered by horrible sores. But Jesus could touch
and love *any* person, no matter how bad they were.
And of course the leper was healed. Wonderful
story. Wonderful Saviour who still touched hearts
and lives today!

As Scotty put the bridle on Rocky he thought
about Aunt Margaret. There was a nagging sen-
sation somewhere inside him that he didn't really
want to admit to himself, and it had to do with his
loving Aunt Margaret as Jesus had loved those who
were not easy to love.

To Scotty's delight, Danny came riding up on
his cream-colored horse Apache just as Scotty was
ready to ride away from the corral. The blond-
haired youth stopped Apache just before the hoofs
came down on a little bushy-tailed gray gopher,
and the boys laughed as the tiny ground squirrel
made a dive into his hole.

"Just about clipped him!" Scotty cried. "Boy,
am I ever glad to see you."

"I told you to call me if anything special happened," Danny reminded with a grin. "What's up?"

"Plenty! But I can't tell you here, because it all has to do with Aunt Margaret." He gazed off toward the distant thunderheads that lay close to the horizon. "Let's ride out past the reservoir where we can talk."

Danny nodded and the fellows pressed their knees against the sides of their horses. Nothing more was needed, and seconds later they were racing along the cattle trail with Butch gamely plugging along behind. Instead of stopping at the reservoir, however, Scotty decided to turn off onto a game trail that climbed high into the hills.

After two miles the land changed rapidly. Instead of so many cacti there were funny little pine trees, great boulders, and signs of deer, coyote, and mountain lion. Quail were in abundance here, as well as cottontail and squirrel. Once in a while they could even glimpse three or four raccoons frolicking over the ground.

Scotty dismounted and tied the reins to a small tree. There was grass here, and Rocky always liked coming up this way. Butch, puffing and grinning, collapsed in a heap and slept.

Danny stood for a moment, letting the cool breeze billow his shirt and dry the sweat from his face. Then he sat down with his knees under his chin and waited for Scotty to begin.

"It started with a doll from Aunt Margaret for Susan," he said. For a moment he was silent, biting his jaw and wondering just how to tell Danny without leaving anything out. Then he dove into the story, watching as his friend's expression turned from laughter to disbelief to bewilderment.

Finally, when the brown-eyed boy had finished, Danny turned eagerly. "You're really serious, aren't you? When you first started talking, I thought you were pulling my leg."

"It really happened," Scotty declared. "All of it."

Danny cocked his head. "Sure is a crazy, mixed-up story. What was that poem again?"

"Let's see— Oh yeah!

A ranch, a cave, a stone;
They're one and yet they're three.
From two and down the river,
Four paces left to the chinaberry tree."

"Wonder what in the world it means," Danny mused softly. "How could a ranch, a cave, and a stone be the same thing?"

"And yet they're three," Scotty added. "And you should have seen that guy, Mr. Karl. He sure was mad at someone!"

Danny lifted both eyebrows. "Too bad."

"What? That Mr. Karl was angry?"

"No, that we'll never know what it's all about,"
Danny turned to look at Scotty. "But you do think
the doll this guy wanted is the same one Susan
has?"

"It has to be. In the first place, the dolls were
all dressed in pink or blue, and there was only one
dressed in red in the whole shipment. In the second place, unless that poem was meant for Mr.
Karl and meant something special to him, why
would he be so furious because the doll was
gone?"

Danny sighed. "Wasn't there anything else?
Some clue? *Something?*"

Scotty shook his head. "No. Mr. Karl —" Scotty's
eyes narrowed, and he snapped his fingers. "Wait
a minute! What was it Mr. Karl said? Something
about— Oh sure, I remember. He said, 'The other
two are worthless without this one.' I'd forgotten
all about that."

Danny's fingers were interlocked so tightly that
they were white. "Other two *what?* Dolls?"

"I don't know." Scotty shrugged. "That's all he
said, except that he was coming back to the store
this afternoon. He just walked out, mad as anything, and that was all."

Silence fell between the boys while they watched
the antics of two squirrels high in the branches of
a cottonwood tree. After a time Danny pulled two

long, brown, leathery-looking things from his pocket and offered Scotty one.

"Jerky?"

Scotty accepted the piece of sun-dried beef and sat chewing the tough, salty end of it. Butch lifted his head, sniffed, and moved closer for his share.

"Ready to go home?"

Scotty pulled himself to his feet. "I guess so. Say, how about staying overnight at the Diamond W?"

"Sounds pretty good. I'll call Mom and see what she says."

"I don't want to be selfish and keep Aunt Margaret all to myself," Scotty grinned.

"Thanks."

They were walking back to their horses when Danny suddenly paused long enough to pull a piece of blue cloth from a catclaw bush. "Someone's missing a piece out of his jacket! Hey, and here on the ground—fresh footprints!"

Scotty took a quick look and shrugged his shoulders. "Probably the guy I saw hunting this morning."

"I haven't heard any gun shots today," Danny said as he swung onto his horse.

Scotty laughed. "Well, maybe he didn't see anything to shoot."

They were closing the gate after putting their

horses in the corral before either of them spoke
again.

"What does your dad have to say about this doll
business?" Danny asked.

"We haven't said anything, because Aunt Margaret is always around and it would probably make
her feel awfully funny. Besides, there won't be
anything more about it, so we may as well forget
the whole thing."

"I suppose so," Danny frowned. "Well, come on,
pal, let's make that phone call so I can share Aunt
Margaret with you."

"You won't think it's so funny two hours from
now," Scotty warned.

Once Danny had the OK from his folks to spend
the night with Scotty, the fellows headed for his
room to wash up for supper. But Scotty hesitated
in his doorway, and his face went blank. Aunt
Margaret had her stuff piled all over the place.

Turning, he stalked to the kitchen where his
mother was busy over the stove. "Mom, Aunt
Margaret's got her things all over my room. I'm
not going to bunk with her."

"Shhh, Scotty!" His mother laid a finger over
her lips quickly. "I was going to put her in with
Susan, but she wanted privacy. So there was nothing to do but give her your room. It's just for two
weeks, son."

"Big deal! Two weeks! So where does that put

me and my things? I suppose if Butch had a dog
house, I'd have to move in with him."

Mrs. Hanson looked at him strangely, and Scotty
felt ashamed of himself. Seemed like he'd felt that
way pretty often since dear old Aunt Margaret
showed up at the ranch.

"The guesthouse isn't more than twenty yards
out the door of your room, Scot. You can clean it
right after supper. It won't be too bad."

The guesthouse! So he was being put out of his
own home. And some guesthouse it was, too.
Sure, a guesthouse for centipedes and tarantulas.
No electric lights or running water. Just a big, old-
fashioned double bed, a tumbledown desk, and a
dresser. *Oh yes, and a kerosene lamp,* he reminded
himself bitterly. He almost forgot that.

"I think it'll be fun," Danny said eagerly. "Some-
times I'd like a little place like that all to myself."

"Well, I wouldn't," Scotty growled.

"Scotty! Son, what's the matter with you?"

"Nothing." He took a deep breath and changed
the tone of his voice. "I'll be OK, Mom. Just a
couple of things getting under my skin, that's all.
Sorry."

Aunt Margaret crooned and twittered all the
way through supper. "You're a dear, sweet boy for
giving me your room, Scotty," she said once.
"You're going to grow up to be a real gentleman.
I just know you are." And with that she reached

over and pinched his cheek. Right in front of
Danny!

Scotty excused himself, and gave the cleaning
of the guesthouse as his reason. Danny dogged
his steps, and Butch followed with his head low,
as though he was sharing in Scotty's embarrass-
ment.

"She almost broke me up," Danny laughed when
they were out of earshot.

"Cut it out."

"Honest, Scotty, I'd die if anyone put me through
that."

"I don't want to talk about it."

Danny swung open the door to the little adobe
house. Mrs. Hanson had opened the windows earlier, but the air was still stale inside. The boys
changed the bed, swept and dusted and even
washed the window by the light of the lamp.

"Old-fashioned," Danny murmured. "I like it."

"Yeah."

"You're really miserable, aren't you, Scot?"

Scotty sighed. "Yeah."

"Why don't you pray about it?"

"Have," Scotty replied shortly.

Danny said no more. He crawled into a pair of
Scotty's pajamas, blew out the light, and opened
the curtains so they'd get some night air. "Do you
want to pray about it now, Scotty?"

Scotty heard the bus stop away down on the

highway and wondered who was getting on at this time of night. He slipped out of bed and knelt on the cold cement floor.

"I guess it would be a good idea," he said at last.

It was very hard to pray for love for his aunt, and when he did, his heart wasn't in it. As a result, when Scotty got up from his knees, he felt worse than he had before. He went to stand at the window, staring toward the darkened glass door of his bedroom.

"I can't figure out what's happened to me since Aunt Margaret came," he said softly. "Everything I do, say, and think is suddenly wrong. I—" He broke off suddenly and reached a hand through the darkness for Danny. "Psst! Come here!"

The two boys stood together by the window, watching as a figure slipped through the moonlight and went to the door of Scotty's bedroom. There it hesitated. Then the person tried the door and found it unlocked. A moment later the figure had entered the bedroom and disappeared!

Chapter Four

RIDE INTO DANGER

DANNY'S HAND felt clammy cold as it encircled Scotty's wrist. "What are you going to do?"

"What *can* we do? If we go through the kitchen and try to get to Mom and Dad's bedroom, we may meet whoever it is right in the hallway. And we can't try to make it through my bedroom, because the person in there may be on his way back out."

They continued to stand there by the window, trembling with excitement. Scotty frowned when the moon slipped under a mass of dark clouds, for now they could not tell when the person came back. A moment later, however, the moonlight was back and shadows played softly over the ground.

Scotty gripped his friend's shoulder. "There he is. *Look!*"

Sure enough, the mysterious black shadow passed silently out of Scotty's room and *came straight toward the guesthouse!* The fellows held their breath in terror. Cold beads of sweat popped out on their faces, and chill bumps rose on their scalps. Still they stood, unable to move or to think of what to do.

Father, Scotty's heart cried out. *Lord, I need You! Show us what to do!*

The figure suddenly hesitated, and Scotty could see that he was a rather short man, not a ranch hand or anything like that. For this man wore a business suit and hat. He stood just outside the window where the boys stood, and he was swearing softly out loud.

"It's got to be here. Sam said the old lady gave this address on the guarantee slip." He moved on a few steps. "If I ever get my hands on the salesman who sold that doll, I'll—"

Scotty could not catch the rest, for the man had disappeared. At least their danger, for the moment, was over.

"Tell me, Scot," Danny whispered. "What was he talking about?"

"I'm trying to put it all together. In the first place, that guy was Mr. Karl. I thought there was something familiar about him. And when he mentioned Sam, I knew who it was. Something else too— I heard a bus stop down on the highway a while ago and wondered who was going aboard. It wasn't anyone getting *on.* It was Mr. Karl getting *off.*"

Danny stroked back his unruly blond hair. "But what did this guy—Mr. Karl—say about a sales slip and this being the address on it?"

"I guess Aunt Margaret had to sign a slip that guaranteed the doll, and she put down this address because she was going to give the doll to Susan. That's how Mr. Karl knew where the doll was." Scotty chuckled. "He sure didn't find it though. He probably looked through all Aunt Margaret's things for the doll, not knowing that it had been given away yet."

"Boy!" The word seemed to explode from Danny's dry lips. "Well, what are we going to do now?"

"I'd like to tell Dad about everything. But we don't know where Mr. Karl is out there. Maybe we'd better just sit tight in here until morning comes."

Danny glanced around. "We could put the desk in front of the door. I don't think the lock works."

"I know it doesn't." There was that odd note of bitterness in Scotty's voice as the realization struck him again that he'd been turned out of his own bedroom just because Aunt Margaret happened to like privacy. "Come on, Danny, but don't make any noise."

After moving the battered old desk in front of the door, the fellows crawled into bed. For a time they lay listening to the night sounds and wondering when one of the sounds was going to come from a human being. There was the gentle *plop*

of an orange dropping to the ground and a rustling
of the wind in the pepper tree. Once Rocky gave
a startled neigh from the corral, and now and then
one could hear the bawling of a steer. After a time
there was an angry rumble of thunder overhead.
The moonlight disappeared, and it became inky
black. Within twenty minutes yellow forks of
lightning spit toward the ground. There was the
sound of rain rustling in the dry palm fronds that
roofed the little porch of the guesthouse.

"Summer rains have started," Danny murmured
softly.

Scotty did not answer but pretended to be asleep
instead. His heart was strangely heavy tonight,
and thoughts of Aunt Margaret surged through
his mind time and time again. He wondered that
one person could bring about such a change in him
in twenty-four hours. Scotty had never realized he
could be bitter and resentful and so full of dislike
for a person. Or was it possible that these awful
things had been in his heart all the time and it
just took someone like Aunt Margaret to make him
see them?

I can't help it, he thought. *I just can't help it!*

"*I can do all things through Christ which
strengtheneth me*," the Holy Spirit reminded gently.

Scotty turned restlessly and prayed desperately
that God would get Aunt Margaret out of his life.

He didn't *like* the way he was feeling. If Aunt Margaret would just go home, then everything would be all right again. And it disturbed Scotty more than he cared to admit that God had never once promised to guide him around a trial. No, God had only promised to see him safely *through* the trials that came his way.

Sleep came sometime during the night. Scotty could not remember getting sleepy, but when he wakened it was to a world washed bright and green and sparkling with a billion raindrops.

The fellows dressed, and Danny declared that he was starving. Scotty picked up an orange on the way to the kitchen and peeled it slowly. Oh, how he dreaded sitting by Aunt Margaret again.

"Well, well," she sang as Scotty entered the kitchen. "And how did my little man sleep last night? It was just the nicest thing you ever did, Scotty, giving me your room."

"I didn't—" Scotty's brown eyes caught his mother's look, and he left the words dangling. "Mom, where's Dad? I've got to talk to him about something real important."

Mrs. Hanson turned slowly. "Well, I believe he's out by the hay shed seeing how much hay got wet last night. That was quite a storm." She hesitated. "Better eat breakfast first, son."

"Do I have to, Mom?" She just had to read what was in his heart.

"Yes, Scotty. You and Danny both see what you can do with this stack of buckwheats! There'll be time enough after that to see your father."

Scotty dropped onto the nearest chair with a sinking feeling in his stomach. Danny joined him.

"We might have been able to track that man if it hadn't rained," he whispered.

Scotty nodded just as he felt a pudgy hand come down upon his head. He winced inwardly and hoped he didn't yell out for Aunt Margaret to take her hand away.

"Scotty, where is the nice train I brought you? I haven't seen you playing with it yet."

You never will, his heart cried savagely.

Aloud he said, "I— I haven't had a chance, Aunt Margaret."

"Well," she laughed, going up and down the scale a couple of times, "I know you like it, and that's what really matters."

"Excuse me, Mom, I've got to find Dad. It's real important— honest!"

"But you didn't finish your breakfast," Aunt Margaret called after him.

"I had enough," Scotty called back over his shoulder.

Danny fell into step with him. "Honest, Scot, how do you stand it? I think I'd either die or holler at her to leave me alone."

Scotty bit his lip. Danny hadn't been saved as

long as Scotty. Somehow Scotty had to act like a
Christian about this thing, no matter what was
going on in the inside. He mustn't let Danny see
how he really felt.

"Did you notice something?" Danny asked.

"What?"

"Aunt Margaret didn't say anything about her
things being messed up. She must not have suspected there was a prowler in her room."

Scotty's brown eyes widened with interest. "Say,
that's right. I suppose that's because the doll was
in a certain size box and Mr. Karl could tell right
off whether it was around or not." Scotty cocked
his head thoughtfully "You can bank on one thing,
though. Mr. Karl hasn't given up finding that doll
as easy as all this."

They were at the hay barn now, and Scotty's dad
was just leaving. He stopped quickly at sound of
the boys' steps.

"Well! How did the two 'guests' sleep last
night?"

Scotty was grim. "I don't think that's very funny,
Dad."

"Well, why not? I think it would be a lot of fun
living out like that. Even with a kerosene lamp
and all." The tall man sat down on a bale of hay.
"What was the trouble?"

Scotty told him the story of Mr. Karl, starting
with Aunt Margaret and the doll and ending with

Mr. Karl entering the house last night. Scotty said nothing about his own personal conflict.

Mr. Hanson's eyes were mirrored with bewilderment. "You kids are really sure about all this? Oh, I know you wouldn't lie to me, Scotty. But it all happened—just the way you told me?"

"Yes sir."

"Well, I'm going to pay Susan's doll a visit, first thing." He stood up. "Don't worry, though. I'm sure, since this Mr. Karl didn't find anything, that he won't be back. I'm still positive it's some kind of a practical joke! But, why don't you ask to stay overnight again, Danny, just so Scotty won't be out in the guesthouse by himself? And I *will* fix that lock this morning."

Now that things were out in the open, Scotty got his chores done in record time, and he and Danny mounted their horses. Maybe they'd just ride over to Danny's place and ask permission for Danny to stay at the Diamond W a little longer.

They started away from the ranch slowly, but the horses felt good after the rain. Soon they were galloping down the trail that led away from the ranch. Scotty had no way of knowing that their every move was being watched through field glasses from far, far away.

Chapter Five

CAVERN OF STRANGE MEN

SCOTTY AND DANNY rode first to the Bar S Ranch and got permission from Danny's mother to stay overnight with Scotty again that night. Danny rolled up a pair of pajamas and some clean socks and underclothing and tied them onto the back of Apache's saddle. Then, with Danny's promise to return home the next morning, the boys rode away.

The desert arroyos were running brimful today, but far off on the distant horizons more dark clouds were beginning to appear. When the clouds rolled together this way from all sides, finally massing in overhead, the land usually had a real gully washer. Yes, the summer rains had begun. Though Arizona was a dry state, it could really have a downpour.

"Are we going straight back to your place?" Danny asked in disappointment.

Scotty shrugged. "We don't have to, I guess. Where do you want to go?"

Danny's gaze wandered away to the jagged mountain peaks in the distance. "We haven't rid-

den up that way for a long time. Remember the
old mine shafts we used to explore? And remember that big old cave where the Diamond W got
its name?"

Scotty smiled. "I sure do. Diamondback Cave.
I also remember how that cave got *its* name. From
all the diamondback rattlers that were once found
there. That place was crawling with snakes."

"But didn't your dad do something to get rid of
all those rattlers about three years ago?"

"He poisoned them, and I suppose they're all
gone. But I still remember when we ran into
those nests of rattlers." Scotty shivered. "It was
awful."

"But, like you say, they're gone now. And it
would be better than going back to face Aunt
Margaret." Danny was grinning, but his voice
held a sober note.

"How true," Scotty echoed, and once more there
was that strange, almost sad, voice whispering
within his heart. Aunt Margaret was old. She
didn't know the Saviour. Scotty must let the love
of Christ be seen in his life, for it was always love
that drew people to the Saviour. And yet all he
could think about was the time when she'd be gone
and life would get back to normal. For, surely, as
soon as she was gone, Scotty would be all right
again. Wouldn't he?

Butch had stayed at home with Susan today,

and Scotty missed being able to look back and see the little bulldog faithfully running along behind Rocky's hoofs.

The horses climbed high where the breeze blew fresh and cool and where the pines grew tall, reaching their boughs to heaven as though in worship to their Creator. Here there were no cacti, no bushy-tailed gophers, and no man-made buildings to spoil the beauty. They were much higher even than yesterday when they had passed the limb of the bush where the hunter had torn his jacket.

"Suppose we'll have a visitor again tonight?" Danny asked.

Scotty shook his dark head. "He won't be back."

"But you said he wouldn't give up that easy."

Scotty frowned. "He won't. But he wouldn't dare keep coming back every single night either, for fear of being caught. He'll probably think up another plan for getting that doll back."

"I'd sure like to know where he went after being in the house last night."

"Wouldn't I?" Scotty agreed. "He must be holing up somewhere. Or else he went back into Tucson to cook up something with Sam."

Danny reined Apache to a halt and swung around in the saddle to look away below him. "You can't even see the ranch from here. In fact, you can't see *any* ranch."

"We're so high that nothing but steers come here. And not many of them. But remember that Diamondback Cave is right on the property line of the Diamond W."

"I didn't remember it being so far," Danny murmured. "And my stomach says it's lunchtime!"

Scotty grinned. "It was your idea, pal. Where's the jerky you always carry in your pocket?"

"At home." Danny groaned. "I forgot to bring some. Juan has been drying some more out by the bunkhouse, so I'll stock up next time for sure." He turned back. "Let's hurry, OK? Take a look at the cave and go back home?"

"Suits me." Scotty pressed his knees gently into Rocky's white sides and thrilled anew at his horse's instant obedience. Boy, despite all the trouble he'd had with Rocky in the beginning, he was certainly a well-trained animal now. Scotty leaned forward and stroked the soft yet powerful neck, and Rocky nickered in return. Again, Scotty felt a great love for his horse welling up in his heart. And Rocky, sensing how his master felt, nickered again and plunged on up the steep path.

They leveled off at last and the boys dismounted. Let's see— the cave was just over to the left, if Scotty remembered correctly.

"I don't see the entrance," Danny said.

"It's got to be here just ahead of us. I— There

it is. Some brush must have blown in front of the opening last night, that's all."

They pulled aside the brush, then hesitated as the whinny of a horse came to their ears. Must be a horse just across the fence, for the sound had not come from Rocky or Apache. Oh well!

Silently they stepped into the murky gloom of the great Diamondback Cave. Strangely, though, instead of stale air rushing out to meet them, Scotty thought sure he smelled smoke! Whether from a cigar or from some kind of a fire, he could not be sure.

This cave went back into the hill for three hundred yards, with two side tunnels branching out from the main tunnel. The cave was not a mine but a natural cavern. The two side tunnels led to rooms big enough to hold a hundred and fifty people, but the main tunnel finally came to a dead end, cut off suddenly by a solid rock wall.

Now that the fellows were here, there really didn't seem to be much purpose for them being here. In fact, Scotty opened his lips to suggest they go back home, when suddenly there came a sound.

His hand whipped out to grasp his friend's wrist. "Listen!"

"I am," Danny whispered. "I heard the sound of a pan rattling."

Scotty removed his boots and took a few steps

forward over the cold, damp stone floor. A pro-
testing Danny followed behind him. Darkness
deeper than any night filled this cave now; but the
boys knew it so well that there was no fear on that
count. The bats singing about their heads were
worse than the darkness.

The *clink-clink* of a coffee pot stopped them
short, however. Now there was no doubt about
there being a small fire somewhere near, for the
smell of coffee was clean and fresh in the damp
air. Probably it was being brewed over canned
heat, for one could not possibly build a fire in this
tunnel.

Trembling and ready to retreat at any second,
the fellows paused at the point where another tunnel branched off to the right. From here they
could hear the sound of voices, rising and falling in
anger.

"So here we sit, Looney. You and me— we got
dolls. But Mr. Karl's doll can't be found, and without the first message the other two are like so much
hash."

Danny grabbed for Scotty's arm. "Looney!
That's the man who works on the Triple B! Next
to the Diam— "

"Shhh!"

"I told you that I know the whereabouts of the
first doll," Mr. Karl explained, much as one would

explain something to a child. "It's just a matter of time."

"Why not contact the man who hid the loot and made up the voice boxes for these dolls? Since we can't seem to trust one another and had Tracey do it, all we have to do is get him from the doll factory and let him tell us where he hid it."

"Look, Taggart," Mr. Karl said quietly, "Tracey was in a car accident three weeks ago. He died instantly."

There was the sound of a man lunging forward. "Why you! You may have had this whole thing rigged. How do we know Tracey is dead? How do we know that doll is really missing? Maybe you know just where this haul is and want to hold out for yourself."

There was the sharp whack of a hand. "Enough! Now, if you men will use your heads, we can get that doll back and all will be well. A cool million won't slip out of Mr. Karl's fingers so easily."

Scotty felt his knees grow weak after Mr. Karl's last statement. Leaving Danny, Scotty crept down the tunnel. The room ahead, where the men were, cut sharply to the left, so he couldn't be seen. There was a light spilling out into the tunnel now, from the room where the men sat drinking coffee and making their plans.

"One million in diamonds, straight from Africa," whispered Looney.

"Well, almost straight," Mr. Karl said quietly. "At least straight from New York where we risked our necks to get them."

Scotty saw something lying on a box just inside the room that caused his pulses to race savagely. He sneaked a quick look. All the men had their backs turned from him. It was daring, dangerous. In one swift, silent move Scotty reached around the corner, snatched the object, and flashed back down the tunnel in his stocking feet.

Laying a trembling hand on Danny's cold wrist, the fellows made a dash for the opening, replaced the brush, slipped on their boots, and sprang into the saddles.

Scotty had thrust the thing he had taken from the cave deeply into the front of his shirt. Now he urged Rocky's sure hoofs down the steep trail and away from the cave. He had to find his dad and tell him what had happened, and he had to see Susan and clue her in.

The boys were in the valley before either of them spoke. Finally Scotty turned a little, his brown eyes almost hidden in the lines of a frown. "That man I thought was a hunter—remember we found a piece of his jacket on a branch? —must have walked from the highway all the way to this cave. Looney must have drawn maps or something for him and Mr. Karl. They decided to meet here—

in Diamondback Cave. Three men and three dolls."

Danny looked strange. "Don't you realize something else, Scot? 'A ranch, a cave, a stone; they're one and yet they're three.' It's a diamond. Diamond W is the ranch, Diamondback Cave is the cave, and the stone, of course, is a diamond too. Or rather, *diamonds!*"

"Why, sure," Scotty said slowly. "And all that adds up to one thing. The diamonds are hidden right here on the Diamond W ranch somewhere."

"It's really something when you get to thinking that your Aunt Margaret brought the first doll to the very place it was supposed to be. Only by accident. It must be driving Mr. Karl crazy to know it's here and he can't find it!"

Scotty smiled. "Yes. The three of them went together and stole the diamonds in New York, but then they had to wait a while till things cooled down. And, because crooks never trust each other, they hired a guy named Tracey to hide the diamonds on the ranch—he probably didn't know how much he had—and make up the talking boxes to put in the dolls. Tracey worked in a toy store up till he died. Now," Scotty went on, grinning broadly, "without the first doll, the men don't know where to start looking."

"Wonder where Sam fits into the picture?" Danny asked.

Scotty reined Rocky to a stop at the split-rail corral and dismounted. Butch had been sleeping under the orange tree not far away where the ground was moist and cool. Now, seeing his master, he hurried forward. His whole stocky little body was wiggling, and he looked guilty.

Scotty knelt to stroke his ears. "Butch, old pal, it's just a good thing for all of us you didn't go along today. One bark and you'd have fouled the whole thing."

Scotty and Danny turned their horses into the corral. Because Rocky was a little sweaty Scotty gave him a quick brush, leaving the hair turned the wrong way so the animal would dry faster. What a horse. How Scotty loved this animal so often termed "loco" in the past.

When Scotty went back to toss the brush into the tack room, he eyes fell once more upon the little New Testament on the shelf. A feeling of guilt swept through him, for today had come and was going and Scotty had not touched his Bible. He had not prayed. He ought to be an encouragement to Danny, who was even younger in the Lord than Scotty.

Soon as Aunt Margaret is gone—

The boys darted to the house with Scotty holding firmly to the front of his shirt. Danny had been eyeing him suspiciously for the last few minutes. But Scotty only smiled and said nothing.

They met Susan hurrying down the hallway from her room to meet them. Her jeans were wrinkled, and her hair was flying.

"I thought you'd never come back," she accused. "And, Scotty Hanson, don't you dare go off again without telling me about the exciting things that are going on! Remember, it was my doll that started this mystery!"

"OK, sis, I promise. Where's Dad?"

"He found a break in the fence west of the ranch. He came back home about an hour ago for tools and a lunch and said he probably won't be home until after dark."

Scotty slapped his forehead with a loud smack. "Oh, that's great!"

"What's the matter?" Susan asked.

Scotty hesitated. "Well, if we stand here, Aunt Margaret is liable to find us. So come on out to *my* place. We've got a lot to tell you, Susan."

The trio sat in the little guesthouse, and Susan listened wide-eyed as the boys unfolded their past adventures. She clasped and unclasped her hands, and once she shivered as from a chill.

"Well, what now, Scotty?" Susan demanded in a hushed whisper. "If those men can't unravel the message without the first one, then we certainly can't do any better without the second and third ones."

"Yes, but you're leaving out something."

"What do you mean, Scot?" Danny frowned.

Scotty had been sitting hunched over. But now he straightened and began to unbutton his shirt. "I," he announced, "have another doll!"

Chapter Six

THE SECOND DOLL

WITH AN AIR OF TRIUMPH, Scotty pulled another doll from his shirt. This one was identical to the one given to Susan, dressed in a red velvet dress and black shoes.

"Where on earth did you get *that?*" Danny gasped.

Susan's blue eyes grew wide with unbelief. "Scotty, that doll is just like mine."

"I got it from the cave. And by now you can guess that it's been missed."

"Those men will be furious," Danny frowned. "Scotty, if they find out that you took this doll, they'll— Well, I don't know *what* they'll do!"

"How can they find out? They don't know we were in the cave. No, I just figure they'll get so nervous, knowing that someone else knows where they are, that they'll scram out of here."

"And leave a whole million dollars' worth of diamonds? Not on your life." Danny's forehead was still furrowed thoughtfully. "Anyway, Scot, what does this doll say? Have you pulled its string yet?"

"I was waiting till we were all together." He reached in back of the doll for the ring. Heart beating with excitement, he pulled the string and waited. The trio sat forward, giving this doll their best attention.

> From the roots of the tree
> To the sandstone wall;
> Into the river
> And under the falls.

There was a rumble of thunder overhead, and Scotty could see through the window that dark clouds were forming once more.

"Pretty smart," Danny nodded. "This Tracey guy who made the voice boxes knew the rainy season would be starting about the time these men met together in Diamondback Cave. That's the *only* time of the year when water would be running anywhere."

"Something else too," Scotty added. "When the river is running there are dozens of little waterfalls that form over the sandstone bluffs. Only the chinaberry tree is the one real clue, and that's why none of the other messages made any sense without the first doll." He turned excitedly. "Because, Susan, the only chinaberry on the whole ranch sits by the river where that old ranch house stood years ago."

Susan snapped her fingers. "That's right! So

the message says from two and down the river. But what's *two?*"

"Well, the cave is the second thing mentioned," Danny reminded. "So wouldn't the cave be two?"

Susan nodded thoughtfully. "Then we'd go from the cave to the river. That would foul them up too," she interrupted herself, "because during rainy season there are lots of rivers. Anyhow we'd go down the river to the chinaberry tree, then to the sandstone wall near the roots of the tree, then into the river and under the falls."

"I never knew of any falls a person could go *under!*" Scotty cried.

"Of course," Danny said, "that country up there is so far from the house here that you don't go up there very often. Maybe the water has washed a hole behind that particular falls. Or maybe a coyote or bobcat has made its home there. Anyway that must be where the diamonds are hidden."

"Yeah," Scotty replied slowly, "but remember that we don't have message number three yet."

"Are you going to tell Mother about all this?" Susan asked.

"I don't think Dad has told her a thing," Scotty objected. "She might be worried. Aunt Margaret might find out too, and if there's one thing we don't want, it's for *her* to find out. She'd jabber endlessly about it."

"Scotty? Why don't we ride up to that river and

take a look around?" Susan's eyes said she was aching to get in on the adventure. "The men couldn't see us from the cave. And if they did, they wouldn't dare try anything. They sure wouldn't kidnap the three of us. The diamonds are too important to bring more trouble on themselves. Besides, they just want to hide out, nice and quiet, until they find what they're after."

Scotty glanced at his watch. "Can't, Susan. It's almost time for supper. Besides, it would be dark before we'd ever get there and back. Maybe in the morning."

"Susan!" It was the voice of Mrs. Hanson from the kitchen doorway. "Come help me with supper, please."

Scotty lifted his brows. "See? But we'll get together after dark, Susan, and lay our plans for tomorrow. I promise. Right now I've got to tend the horses for the night."

Susan started out of the guesthouse, but paused in the doorway with her hands on her hips. "What about the two dolls? We'd better bury them or something."

"I'll hide them under the bed in here. Mr. Karl would never think of looking there. Besides, he has no idea there's anyone living in here."

"That's fine," Susan said, "but what am I going to do if Aunt Margaret wants to know where my doll is?"

Scotty bit his lip. What Susan said was all too true. And, knowing his aunt, she'd want to know, all right!

"Why not take out the voice box and hide it?" Danny suggested. "Then just leave the doll where it is."

Scotty nodded quickly. "That's it! We'll take out both voice boxes and hide them so Mr. Karl will never find them. That's a great idea."

Scotty went out to the corral to take care of the horses for the night. He was stroking Rocky and allowing the great white horse to nip lovingly at his ear when Aunt Margaret appeared on the scene.

"Scotty, I do believe that you have the nicest horse I've ever seen. Do you know that I've been visiting Rocky lately with an apple or piece of carrot, and he's beginning to know just who I am!"

Once he saw you, how could he ever forget? Scotty thought, and then the misery in his heart deepened and he wished Aunt Margaret would just go home where she belonged. It came to him with great shock that Aunt Margaret's presence here on the ranch had actually stepped between him and God. That was the reason for his misery. It was conviction brought by the Holy Spirit. But how did a guy love a woman like Aunt Margaret?

Pray, a voice said gently. *"For every one that asketh receiveth."*

"— I guess my horse is real smart that way," he stammered. "Rocky's real great."

"And so are you, Scotty!" his aunt purred. "The way you've trained your horse is just wonderful." She went toward the white horse. "Rocky, look what I have for you." And she held out a piece of red apple.

Scotty turned away. "I'll— I'll see you at the house, Aunt Margaret."

After supper that night Scotty and Danny worked feverishly, removing the voice boxes and hiding them in a far corner under the old dresser in the bunkhouse. Then Susan took her doll back to her room, with the promise that she'd hide it safely away during the night.

Scotty took the second doll and buried it deep under the soft dirt under the pepper tree. It was dark now, and there was no moon in sight. Instead, the clouds which had been gathering all day were beginning to send forth great drops of rain that struck the flesh and then spattered. A whopping big storm was in the making, and that was certain.

By the time Mr. Hanson drove to the ranch in the battered little jeep, it was pouring rain. Tongues of lightning shimmered against the earth, and a hard wind lashed through the trees and tore off branches. Thunder louder than anything Scotty had ever heard rumbled and crashed across the heavens. And all the time, though no one knew it, a tragedy was beginning to happen.

Chapter Seven

DOUBLE DISAPPEARANCE

IT WAS AFTER MIDNIGHT when the rain slackened and the lightning and thunder passed over into the distance. The desert was green and sparkling as the moon once again shone brightly over the land. Horses and cattle stood with bowed heads, their hides wet and smelly. The only sound to break the strange hush that had fallen over the ranch was the lusty crowing of a rooster that had ventured forth. And this sound was strange too, because it was not the hour for a rooster to crow.

Though the storm had served to lull Danny into deep slumber, Scotty was still tossing restlessly. He'd tried every position in the books. Now he lay staring up at the darkened ceiling of the little guesthouse. *Lousy bed,* he thought. *If I were in my own bed, I bet I'd sleep.*

He tried thinking about the two mysterious messages. He wondered what the third one said and if he'd ever find out. He took an imaginary ride on Rocky. They galloped, harder, harder, harder, until they flew past the twisting giant *sahuaros* where the wind sang about the cactus needles and where the hills rolled wild and free.

But still sleep would not come. Getting up, Scotty paced to the window. The stars were popping out again, winking and shining for the glory of God.

God. . . .

Scotty ducked his head and blinked a few times. His jaw was tight and his lips pressed firmly together. Yes, that was his trouble. God wanted to speak to Scotty's heart, and the boy had not given the Holy Spirit the right to speak. He'd kept his mind so busy that God could not speak to him. But now it was time to face facts. Now it was time to get alone with God and face *himself*. That was the hardest of all, facing Scotty Hanson and the way he'd acted and felt lately.

Gritting his teeth, Scotty stuck his bare feet into his slippers and unlocked the door of the guesthouse. Alone and lonely, he slipped out into the moonlight.

Funny, how lonely he could feel when he wasn't aware of the presence of God. How terribly empty life would be without the Son of God. What was there, really, without the Lord Jesus Christ? Who could Scotty talk to when he was lonely? Or tell his troubles to? Who would comfort him when he was sad? Or put a song in his heart when life grew dark all around? Or *give him victory in his heart when trials pressed in?*

Tears came to the boy's eyes as the Holy Spirit began to deal with him. Yes, Aunt Margaret had caused him a great trial. But getting Aunt Margaret out of the picture and off the ranch wasn't really the answer. Sure, that would take Scotty around the trial and out of it, but he'd come out no stronger spiritually than before. No, the only way to have victory in this matter was to conquer right where he was. With Aunt Margaret still here, Scotty must give himself to Christ so completely that Jesus Himself would live through Scotty's life and win this battle. After all, Jesus loved Aunt Margaret and yearned for her to see herself as a sinner in need of the Saviour. Jesus wanted Aunt Margaret to come to Him for salvation. And He wanted to use Scotty's life in this thing somehow. Certainly He wanted Scotty to come through this trial stronger than he went into it.

"I beseech you therefore, brethren, by the mercies of God, that ye present your bodies a living sacrifice, holy, acceptable unto God, which is your reasonable service."

"Romans twelve, verse one," Scotty murmured softly. He looked up toward the dazzling stars, then at the moon. All these and more God the Creator had flung into being. All these He kept there by His mighty power. Surely then His power was great enough to keep Scotty and bring him through this thing, not with hatred and bitterness in his heart, but with the love of Christ shining there.

"Do it for me, heavenly Father," he whispered. "Do it all through my life. Let me be everything You ever wanted me to be. I want to give You my best."

With these words a great peace came to Scotty's heart. How wonderful that forgiveness was his through the blood of Jesus! Oh, the world was a great place tonight—washed clean, as his heart was washed clean.

And, returning to the guesthouse, Scotty slept.

When Danny tried to rouse his friend at 8:00 the next morning, Scotty simply grunted and turned over.

"Hey, pal, wake up," the blond-haired youth insisted. "I've got something to tell you!"

Scotty grunted again, but this time he struggled to sit up. "Why the rush? What's the matter?"

"Your dad got in late last night, and about daylight this morning he got in the car and drove away."

Scotty swung his legs over the side of the bed and thrust his feet into his slippers. "What's wrong with that? He probably had to see one of the other ranchers about something."

Danny shook his head. "Huh-uh! He was dressed

in his best suit and boots, and he kissed your mother good-bye. He acted like he was leaving for a while. In fact, he even had some sort of a case with him—maybe an overnight case or something."

By now Scotty was wide awake. "But we have to tell him about those men in Diamondback Cave!" Hurriedly, Scotty pulled on his shirt and jeans and forced his feet into his boots. He was pulling his belt through the loops of his jeans as he went out the door.

Aunt Margaret began to croon as soon as Scotty opened the kitchen door, and Scotty was surprised and glad that he could smile and say good morning to her.

"Say, Mom, Danny said Dad left a while ago. He's coming back in a little while, isn't he?"

Scotty's mother broke an egg into the skillet before answering. "They've called a special meeting of the Cattlemen's Association and your father, being vice-president, had to attend. He'll be in Phoenix overnight." She glanced at Scotty and smiled. "Well, don't look so gloomy. The rest of us are still here, and Danny will be staying overnight again. Three nights in a row is pretty good!"

Scotty grinned. "Sure it is, Mom. Only I had something real important to tell Dad."

"Your father had wanted to talk to you too, son,

but he had to leave so early. He did leave a message for me to give you though."

The dark-eyed boy looked up quickly. "Yes?"

She turned the egg slowly. "Well, it doesn't make any sense to me at all, but perhaps it will to you. He said to tell you not to worry about the other night, that he was sure everything was all right. He said to be sure and use the thing he fixed in the guesthouse and to tell Susan to put away the thing you had talked to him about earlier."

Scotty nodded slowly. "I understand, Mom." He looked at Danny quickly and caught his look of understanding. Scotty's father wanted him to lock things up tonight and he wanted Susan to hide the doll. Well, that had already been taken care of, so now all Scotty could do was pray that the Lord would take care of the Diamond W and those who lived there.

After breakfast Scotty headed for the corral. Butch, rested from the last long run, seemed ready to go again. He trotted along so close behind Scotty that a couple of times he stepped on the boy's boot heels. Tongue hanging and grinning from ear to ear, Butch was one black and white ball of eagerness.

Scotty ducked under the pepper tree, cupped his hands about his mouth and called, "Rock-ee-ee!"

This morning there was no answering neigh, no thunder of hoofs coming to the gate to greet him. Scotty dashed forward a few yards, sure of hearing his horse whinny a greeting by that time, only to be met by dead silence. It was then he saw that the corral gate was standing wide open.

Danny stared at Scotty for a moment before both boys ran forward. Most of the other horses were in the corral, though three were grazing contentedly just outside the gate. But Rocky was nowhere in sight.

Scotty lifted his voice again and again calling out to his great white horse, but there was no answer.

"He's got to be around somewhere nearby," he said slowly. "Come on, Danny, let's scout around for him." But two questions hammered over and over through his brain. Who had left the gate open? Why didn't Rocky answer?

They rode bareback this morning, Scotty riding a mare known as Chiquita, which means "little girl" in Spanish. But though they rode high into the hills and explored every little canyon, Rocky did not appear. A feeling of foreboding crept into Scotty's heart—and *this* right after last night's wonderful meeting with the Lord! How easy it had seemed last night, when God was so near, to believe it would be easy to live *above* the storms of life. When the storm struck, however,— Well, that was the real test!

"Let's go back," Scotty suggested after two hours. "Probably Rocky is right back in the corral wondering where *I* am."

Danny laughed. "I sure hope so. How'd you happen to leave that gate open last night, Scotty?"

"I didn't," Scotty frowned. "I've fed and watered the horses too many times to do a thing like that!"

Danny cocked his blond head. "But you were the last one in the corral."

Scotty sighed. He had been there, all right. He'd told Rocky good— *Wait!* Aunt Margaret had come with an apple for Rocky. She was the last one in the corral. And she wasn't used to being with horses or shutting corral gates. *She* was the one who had left the gate open. Oh boy, what an awful turn this thing was taking.

As the boys neared the ranch Scotty's keen eyes searched through the horses in the corral, but he could not pick out a pure white horse with a silken mane and a flowing tail.

"He'll be back," Scotty muttered half under his breath. "I know he'll be back pretty soon. But, just in case, let's fill a canteen. And if Rocky's not back home in an hour, we'll go out again."

Danny nodded. Butch, having gone all this way with the fellows, fell down in the shadow of the orange tree and lapped water from the hose that lay running nearby. Clearly he was finished for the day!

"Scot!"

Scotty looked up quickly. His mother seldom called him "Scot" unless there was something wrong. "Yes, Mom?"

"Son, would you come to the house?"

He looped the reins over the corral fence and turned. "Sure, Mom."

Mrs. Hanson was still standing in the open doorway of the kitchen when Scotty got there. Her hands were trembling and her eyes looked as if she'd been crying.

"Mom? What's the matter, Mom?"

"Scotty, it's— it's about your horse." She turned away, biting at her lower lip nervously. "Come in the house, Scotty."

Terror streaked through Scotty's pulses. He felt light-headed and numb. "Something's wrong with Rocky?"

He sat down on the stone hearth in front of the fireplace and let his hands drop loosely between his knees. "Tell me what's wrong, Mom! Where is my horse?"

Aunt Margaret was standing in the doorway looking worried and sick, and behind her was Susan's blond head. She couldn't even look at her brother.

Mrs. Hanson sat down near Scotty. "Son, Rocky must have wandered away during the night. The rains have brought a good crop of grass, you know,

and Rocky most likely was taking advantage of it."
She paused, and Scotty knew she was wishing that
his father was here to break the news. "Scotty,
Mr. Williams called a half hour ago. He—he found
a white horse that—that had been struck by a
loaded semitruck during the night."

Scotty felt his face sag, and he thought he was
going to faint. "How—how badly is he hurt, Mom?"

"Scotty, he's—*dead.*"

Scotty raced to his feet and headed for the door.
"It's not Rocky! Mom, I know it can't be Rocky!
Please, Mom, take me to him!"

Her hands fell upon his shoulders. "Scotty,
Susan and I drove down to the Williams' ranch a
few minutes ago. You—you wouldn't want to see
your horse, Scot, the—the way he is now. Try to
accept this as from the Lord, son. Though it's hard
to give up a horse that's become a part of your
life, God does know best!"

Hot, flashing anger suddenly welled up within
Scotty's heart. With clenched fists he turned to his
aunt. "You did this!" he accused. "You left the
gate open last night! It's your fault my horse is
dead!"

Aunt Margaret was crying softly. "I know that,
Scotty. I'll buy you another horse! I'll—"

"I don't *want* another horse! I'll never want another horse!" He almost cried out that things had

been wrong ever since she'd been here, but dashed from the house instead.

Blindly, Scotty ran into the desert and over the hills, throwing himself down in exhaustion at last. Tears coursed down his face freely now that he was alone, and Butch, frightened and bewildered by his master's strange behavior, nestled close and buried his cold nose against Scotty's neck.

I hate her! he thought. *I hate Aunt Margaret for doing this to me!*

Let me be everything You ever wanted me to be. I want to give You my best.

Was it only last night when he'd told his heavenly Father this? Last night and not a hundred years ago? How could things change so fast? How could it be that in a few short hours Scotty was worse spiritually than he'd ever been before? Oh, what was the matter with him?

Struggling to his feet, Scotty began to walk. He didn't know how far, and he didn't care. He couldn't pray, because he couldn't face God with his failure. And he couldn't go home because he couldn't face anyone there. Scotty felt as if he'd been caught in a whirlpool and there was no way out of it.

He had reached the rim of scrubby pines and giant boulders when he stopped and lay down upon a bed of pine needles. It was cool here, for a gentle breeze was blowing. Above, great white

thunderheads moved lazily to the south, and beneath them a buzzard circled slowly.

Rocky! What if that buzzard was after Rocky?
Oh, but no, for a truck would take him away and—
And there Scotty dared think no further. His heart
broken and crushed with pain that was almost un-
bearable, he tried desperately not to sob again.

Gone was the mystery that had so taken his attention. Gone was Diamondback Cave and its
strange men! It didn't matter. Nothing mattered
except that the horse he'd raised from a little
scrawny white colt that everyone said was loco
was gone from his life. It left a spot that was
empty and lonely.

Then very slowly Scotty was aware of other
things. He realized sharply how he must have
grieved the heart of God in acting the way he had
to Aunt Margaret. And he realized that Christ
could fill the loss he felt so keenly, if Scotty would
let Him.

Slowly Scotty sat up. "Please, God, forgive me
again. Seems like I've had to ask You to forgive
me a lot lately. You know, Father, You know more
than anyone how much I loved Rocky. But I know
I can't love him or anyone—or anything—more than
I love You! You've got to have first place in my
life, Lord Jesus, because I truly *do* love You best."
Scotty bit his lip for a moment. "Lord, help me to
go home and face Aunt Margaret and—and ask he

to forgive me too. I failed You, but help me to go back again."

With this, Scotty started for home. Yes, he'd failed because he'd taken things into his own hands instead of letting the Lord handle things His way. Oh, if Scotty could only learn to give himself so completely to the Lord that Jesus would be living His own life through Scotty. Only then could Scotty truly speak and act in love.

It was nearly 3:00 that afternoon before Scotty finally dragged his weary body to the house. Susan was waiting for him in the yard, and she was wearing a frown as dark as the gathering clouds in the north.

"You sure fixed things, Scotty!"

"I know it." He punched a hole in the earth with the toe of his boot. "I came home to apologize."

"It's too late," Susan sighed.

"What do you mean?"

"Aunt Margaret. She said she was going to the mailbox for the mail, and she never came back. She just left a note there that she had messed everything up and had decided to catch the bus for town. By now she's on her way to Ohio."

Chapter Eight

UNDERGROUND RIVER

SCOTTY STOOD IN FRONT of his sister, dazed and bewildered. "What are you talking about?" he gasped finally. "Aunt Margaret gone? Gone where?"

"Gone home, goofy!" Susan gave a toss of her blond hair. "Scotty, I know it was an awful blow about Rocky, and we all feel just terrible about it. But what you did to Aunt Margaret was pretty terrible too."

"I know. And I did come back to apologize! Honest, I did, Susan!" Scotty fell into step with his sister as they headed for the house. "But, Susan, how could Aunt Margaret take a bus for Ohio from here? And what about her clothes and stuff?"

"She left a note at the mailbox and asked us to ship her things. She either must have caught the bus for town and gone on from there, or else she caught the eastbound Greyhound and went right on through Tucson."

Scotty's heart was hammering, and he was trembling. It was too much all in one day. It was just too much.

"Did Mom call the bus station in Tucson? Maybe she can catch her at the depot."

"She called, all right, and found out that four minutes after the bus gets to Tucson there is another bus leaving for the East. And, knowing that she might have already taken a cross-country bus, we knew we couldn't possibly catch her at the bus station." Susan took a deep breath and let it out slowly as she talked. "No, Aunt Margaret is gone, and that's that!"

Scotty ducked his head. "Did—was she really hurt pretty badly over—over what I said?"

"She was crushed, Scotty. She thought you were the only star in her sky. So when you turned on her, it was more than she could bear. I felt sorry for her."

Scotty felt sorry too—for Aunt Margaret, for Rocky, and for himself. He was hurt over Rocky, but he was just plain mad at himself for talking to Aunt Margaret the way he had. Poor old lady, and not even having the Lord to lean on. What was the matter with him anyway? He'd bite out his tongue if it would do any good! Why, he might never see his aunt again. She might never come to know the Lord Jesus now. And suddenly Scotty realized that he was truly concerned about this aunt he'd thought he hated!

No one had much to say that night. It was lonely on the Diamond W without Mr. Hanson, for his huge presence always filled the house with laughter and cheer.

Scotty's mother was gently reproving, though she and Scotty had had a serious talk earlier. After that his mother, for the most part, was quiet. After all, it had been her sister that Scotty had shocked and hurt so bitterly.

Danny too was thoughtful and quiet. Only Susan was openly voicing her various opinions on the goings-on at the ranch.

Scotty wished his mother would whale the tar out of him. He wished she'd put him to bed without supper. He deserved the worst, and anything would have been better than this awful silence.

But they all knew that Scotty, too, was suffering over the loss of his horse, and it was that one thing that caused them to begin to understand his behavior.

It was with a heavy heart that Scotty and Danny moved back into the house that night. Scotty wondered why God had brought him to the place where he was willing to apologize to Aunt Margaret, only to discover that she was gone from the Diamond W. Was it because the Lord had only wanted Scotty to be *willing?* Or was it, somehow, more than that? Of course, he could write all the way back to Ohio, but somehow that wasn't as good as doing it in person. He sighed. Well, he'd write, anyway, and do the very best he could.

Because Scotty was so exhausted, sleep came quickly. But with sleep came troubled dreams. They were dreams where a wet, stringy-looking white colt stood on its matchstick legs and wobbled back and forth. It was a dream where men wanted to shoot and kill a horse they called loco, but where time and time again the horse had refused to die.* It was a dream where Scotty mounted the beautiful animal in a plowed field for the first time, and again he tasted the thrill and wonder of it. Yes, it was a dream where a horse with hoofs of thunder and eyes of fire galloped over the trails, through the deep boulder-choked canyons, and up where the wind rushed through the trees wild and free. A horse that lay broken and crushed by a great truck rushing headlong through the night.

Scotty sat up with a start and found his pulses racing and his eyes staring. Not Rocky!

"No!"

"Scot? Are you OK, pal?"

Scotty shuddered as he slipped out of bed. He couldn't break down, not in front of Danny.

"I-I'm OK, Danny."

Going to the window, he stood for a long time gripping the windowsill and trying to drive back the tears. There was no friendly whinny in the corral tonight. No, nor ever again. No white horse

*See *Scotty and the Horse That Wouldn't Die.*

would be in the corral in the morning. Nor the next, nor the next, nor ever again. Once and for all Scotty had to face the fact that Rocky was gone.

"It's rough, Scotty," Danny said quietly from the shadows.

"Yeah."

"It could just as easily have been Apache. I was thinking that today."

"But it wasn't." Scotty turned around slowly. "I'm glad it wasn't Apache, Danny. I want you to know that. But I sure wish it—it hadn't been my horse either."

"So do I, Scotty!"

After a while Scotty slipped back into bed. God would heal the wound in time. He had to remember Aunt Margaret and pray for her. She'd probably always blame herself for Rocky's death.

"We'll ride up into the hills in the morning," Danny said. "It will help if you keep your mind busy."

"Sure it will." Scotty leaned down and scratched Butch's ears. "Thanks, Danny."

The rest of Scotty's dreams that night were filled with a boy who struck out at an old woman, saying things to her that should not be said. He saw the hurt look that crossed the woman's face, the pain and bewilderment. He saw that the old woman had no one to turn to, though the boy could flee into the hills and cry out to a Saviour who loved, understood, and helped. And the boy was Scotty.

Morning brought little relief. Scotty's father would not return to the ranch until late afternoon. Mrs. Hanson was going into town for a bit of shopping, though Scotty strongly suspected that it was more to get her mind off things for a while than for any other reason.

"I think I'll stay home today," Susan said when invited to go along. "Scotty and Danny have promised to let me ride with them today, and this is so unusual I don't dare miss the chance."

"I'll be home around two this afternoon," Mrs. Hanson said as she went out the door. "There's meat in the refrigerator for sandwiches and fruit on the table. Don't forget to take care of the—" She broke off suddenly, bowed her head, and finished lamely, "—horses."

Alone, the trio wasted no time. While Scotty saddled Susan's horse, she made sandwiches for all of them. By the time the fellows were ready, Susan emerged triumphantly from the house with a huge lunch ready to stick inside the saddlebag.

"We'll follow the directions just as we have them," Danny decided. "Since we already know where the cave is—and that's the starting point— we'll head for the river just below the cave and hope it's not running so full that we can't cross it.

Then we'll find the chinaberry tree and go from there."

Susan laughed. "Those men don't have a chance without the first message."

Scotty gazed longingly from the corral in back of him to the mare he was riding. Would he ever get used to riding this horse? Could any horse ever take Rocky's place? No. There wasn't a horse on earth that could take Rocky's place in Scotty's heart.

Following the game trail high into the mountains, they crossed many streams, swollen now from the past rains. Instead of going on up to the cave, however, and running the risk of being detected, they stopped at the river. Though it had been running full, it was down now to a muddy creek that ran pell-mell over rocks and weeds, ever making its way to the Rillito River miles away.

"Now to the chinaberry tree," Susan announced. She reined her horse upstream. "We certainly won't have any trouble finding *that!*"

"Being the only one on the ranch," Danny murmured drily, "I suppose not."

They traveled slowly along the river, for boulders choked the banks. And where these did not exist the riverbanks were soft and crumbly. If the horses went too near, the ground could give way beneath the hoofs and they'd be plunged into the rushing muddy water. They traveled for two miles this way, and finally Susan paused and pointed to a mesa across the river.

"There's the old foundation to the house," she said. "And there's the chinaberry tree, green as can be and blooming for all it's worth."

Sure enough, a towering chinaberry tree stood beside the river. It was big enough to shade an entire house and yard, had there been a house and yard there to shade. Its top was covered with lovely purple flowers that spilled out their fragrance into the moist air.

"And there are the roots," Danny exclaimed. "See, the tree is so close to the river that the rushing water has uncovered some of its roots."

Scotty was silent during this time. The thrill of adventure was gone, and in its place was a kind of dread. He wished—and tried not to wish—for many things. He knew the things he wished for could never be. He felt himself to be simply a kind of silent partner in this adventure, nothing more. Even a treasure in diamonds could not lure him now.

"The second poem said—" Susan put a finger under her chin and thought for a moment. "Let's see. 'From the roots of the tree to the sandstone wall.'" She turned in the saddle. "That's the closest sandstone wall across from the tree on this side of the river. But it certainly isn't a very big wall."

Every eye turned to the sandstone bluff ahead
of them. Farther away were more bluffs like this
one, but this was indeed the nearest one. They
moved forward.

The sound of rushing water came to their ears,
and as they came around the bend in the river a
beautiful, cascading waterfall met their gaze. They
had seen many smaller waterfalls today, but this
one was bigger and lovelier.

"The guy who made the directions sure must
know this country, because if the rainy season
wasn't here that thing would be bone dry." Danny
grew sober. "Only thing is, the message said, *under* the falls."

"Let's cross the river, Danny," Scotty suggested,
"and take a look for ourselves."

Susan quickly dismounted and tied her horse.
"You're not going without me, Scotty Hanson! My
doll started all this, remember?"

"I remember," Scotty replied listlessly.

The trio crossed the river by stepping from rock
to rock. There was but a narrow shelf of rock beside the waterfall, and they stepped onto this gingerly. Scotty peeked behind the water.

"It's dark, like a hole of some kind. Seems like I
remember seeing it once before, but I always
thought it was just a cave where some animal
lived."

"We're going to be soaked!" Danny declared. "Want me to go first?"

Scotty took a deep breath. "No, I'll go first. Give me the light, Danny."

Danny had looped the saddlebag containing their lunch and the flashlight over his shoulder before starting across the river, and now he dug through it for the light.

Scotty eased his body through the slight opening behind the falls, and the roar and tumble of it filled his ears. It was eerie and dark back here with a curtain of water falling in front of his face. And what do you know! It looked like a cave from outside, but here Scotty could see that it was a narrow tunnel that dipped down sharply and then, seemingly, went on and on. He turned the light around slowly, gasping when he saw water rolling along at the bottom of the little hill.

"Hey, Danny!" he yelled. "Susan! I think we've found an underground river!"

Chapter Nine

THE PRISONER

LOOKING BACK, about all Scotty could see was the rushing waterfall. The spray from it hit his face and dampened his clothing. He felt the sides of this strange place. As he remembered this wild part of the country, this opening had been so small that only an animal could make its den here. That was the reason Scotty had never bothered to explore, for there were too many old mine shafts and caves on the ranch to bother with one so small. But now! Why, the opening was five feet high in one spot. The rains must have washed away the dirt and rocks and opened this place up.

A hand reached around the opening, then a foot, and a moment later Danny had leaped into the opening with Scotty. He put the bag with the sandwiches on the ground and reached out to help Susan.

"I don't know what good this will do," he said. "We still don't know where to go from here without the third message."

Susan made a wild dive behind the wall of water, but she managed to soak her flying blond hair anyway. "What's the roaring noise in here?" she whispered.

"Some kind of an underground river," Scotty answered softly. "Come on, I'll show you!"

They passed under a ledge of rock where the light revealed a cluster of bats hanging upside down, and Susan let out a cry of fright. The sound carried far down the tunnel and then bounded back with several clear echoes.

"Don't yell," Scotty whispered, "no matter what! Sound carries like anything."

"Well, there's no one here but us," Susan replied indignantly.

"I know, but just the same, don't yell! It's weird enough in here without echoes flying all over the place." The truth was, Scotty admitted to himself, he was real edgy today. It helped a lot to do something and try to keep himself busy, but his thoughts turned constantly to Rocky. From Rocky they turned to Aunt Margaret and then back to Rocky until it got pretty well confusing.

The bats, disturbed, loosened their hold of the rock and went flying through the tunnel. Their wings sang in the still air. Susan pressed the back of her hand to her lips, but she did not cry out.

They passed down the steep slope to the edge of the rapid stream below. Scotty played the light up and down, and his brown eyes almost popped with unbelief when he saw the small, flat aluminum boat twenty feet away!

"Do I see what I *think* I see?" Danny cried in a whisper. "Can there be a *boat* in here?"

Scotty passed a hand over his forehead. "Boy, I feel like I left the Diamond W far behind and have stepped into another world somewhere. How can there be an underground stream, much less a boat? And why? Where did it come from anyhow?"

"Well," Susan began hesitantly, "the message guides us to this spot, so that means this man Tracey was here long ago—before he ever made those messages. If he brought in a lightweight boat, then he must have *gone somewhere* in it."

Scotty frowned. "That's right. Question is, where could this stream go that a person would need a boat?" His dark eyes were asking another question. *Do we dare find out?*

"We don't know where to go from here," Danny said quietly, "but I'd hate to think that we came all this way and didn't at least find out where the stream goes!"

"Yes," Scotty murmured.

"It sounds awfully dangerous," Susan put in.

"But there is a little ground on this side of the stream," Danny went on. "If anything happened, all we'd have to do is follow the stream back. And it doesn't look too deep."

It was with great hesitation, however, that the

trio stepped into the tiny boat. An even greater feeling of dread crept into their hearts when the little boat sank deeper into the water.

"This boat was made for one person, I can tell you that," Danny grinned. "But if we sit still I think it will be all right."

Scotty untied the rotted rope that was anchored to a protruding rock. Then the three young people sat stiffly in the middle of the little boat to keep it from rocking. With the water lapping gently on the metal sides, the boat began to move. Though the current was slight, yet there was enough movement in the water to send the boat slowly along.

Scotty held the light tightly, shining its beam before them. With the darkness so thick, however, the light did little to pierce it. Twice he flashed the light toward the edge of the water to make certain there was still a little ledge of rock to walk back on if they had to.

For five minutes they moved along in this fashion. Foot by foot, the water carried them forward. Except for the splash of water and the singing wings of a bat, all was perfectly quiet.

"Seems like we ought to be somewhere else," Danny murmured. "In Africa maybe on a jungle stream, or in South America moving down the Amazon at night. Anywhere but in Arizona!"

Scotty was in no mood for make-believe. He was brooding over Rocky's terrible death and over his actions toward poor old Aunt Margaret who was lost without the Lord Jesus Christ. And very slowly, though Scotty did not realize it then, he was growing far more concerned for his aunt's salvation than he was for Rocky's death.

One thing still puzzled Scotty greatly. Why had God so convicted Scotty that he had come back to the ranch to apologize to Aunt Margaret, only to find that she was gone? Surely God knew that she would not be there when Scotty arrived.

Here I go, getting back on that merry-go-round, he thought. *And I don't have any answer, so there's no sense thinking about it.*

One thing Scotty did know, and that was that God had forgiven him for his past failures. His heavenly Father knew that he wanted God's will for his life above what Scotty himself wanted, and somehow, in some way, God was doing an unseen work in Scotty's life. He just had to believe it, that was all.

The deeper they traveled through this strange tunnel the damper it grew. The smell of staleness was everywhere.

"Shine the light over here," Susan asked.

Scotty swept the beam of light to the side, and the trio was startled to discover that the edging of rock beside the water was gone. The entire tunnel was filled with water now, and it gave them an eerie feeling to be closed in like this. When they spoke, their voices bounced back quickly from the stone walls.

Scotty had heard of a place something like this outside the town of Oracle, Arizona, where a cave had been discovered with a great lake inside. Why, in that place the Navy had even sent down skin divers, and they had not yet found the bottom. He wondered if this stream would stop pretty soon, ending up at some great underground lake.

And suddenly, as though in answer to his thoughts, the river did end. Not, however, as they had expected. The stream made a turn, and the ceiling lowered until it was impossible for them to stay in the boat. To Scotty's left was a hole through the rock, barely big enough for a person to crawl through. And through this hole shone a pale light.

Susan opened her lips to say something, and Danny quickly clapped his hand over her mouth. "Shhh! Don't say a word."

Trembling and frightened, Scotty slipped out of the boat and into the icy water. He was thankful to find that it wasn't quite waist-deep. Steadying the boat, he stopped to look through the hole and into the underground chamber on the other side

What he saw caused him to choke back the cry of surprise and alarm. Just inside the strange rock chamber ahead of him within arm's reach was a box. It was bigger than a shoe box, and lying in the folds of white tissue paper was a talking doll in a red velvet dress!

Stooping still lower, he peered through again. A moment later the blood drained from his face, and his jaw dropped open. He reached back a cold hand to grasp his sister's arm. It couldn't be. But it was. *That was Aunt Margaret in there, tied hand and foot!*

Chapter Ten

THE THIRD MESSAGE

SCOTTY SUCKED in his breath hard. He looked again to be sure his eyes weren't somehow playing tricks on him. But even by the pale yellow light of the lantern Scotty could see that it was truly Aunt Margaret.

Her eyes were wide and frightened. There was a dirty red and white handkerchief tied over her mouth. She sat against the rock wall of the underground room, and her wrists were tied behind her. Her legs were stretched out in front of her and they, too, were secured by a cord.

The three men were nowhere in sight, and it was a great temptation to enter the room. He could free Aunt Margaret and get the doll and—

And what? Aunt Margaret could never in a lifetime squeeze through the little opening in front of Scotty! No, that wasn't the answer. There had to be some other way!

Very, very slowly Scotty turned in the waist deep water and began guiding the boat back down the stream. His only hope was that there were no sudden drop-offs!

"What's the—?"

"Shhh!"

They used no light, and the blackness was thick about them. Once Scotty bumped the boat into the side of the tunnel and he paused in terror. Nothing happened. Only the lapping water and the steady *drip-drip* of water into the stream from above broke the stillness. Of course, Scotty had to remember that the men did not know about this stream. They were too big to enter it by way of the little hole in the rock wall. And since the first message guiding them by way of the chinaberry tree was missing, they had no way of knowing anything about this place!

When the boat was to the place where Scotty could force it upon the narrow edge of rock, he sank back with a deep sigh. Turning on the light, he played it over the area where they sat. Everything was all right.

"Scotty, what could you have seen that scared you so much?" Susan asked in a whisper.

"I saw Aunt Margaret!" he replied quickly.

"You saw—*Aunt Margaret?*"

"Yes! She didn't leave the ranch at all. She must have gone for the mail, and Mr. Karl forced her to write that note and leave the ranch with him. After all, he knew that she bought the doll he was supposed to pick up. And he didn't find it the night he went into the house, so he had to get Aunt Margaret herself and try to force her to tell him what she did with the doll."

Susan's eyes grew wide in the pale light. "I wonder if she did," she gasped.

"I can hardly believe it!" Danny whispered hoarsely. "Mr. Karl *kidnapped* your aunt! Boy, what a penalty there is for kidnapping."

"Yes," Scotty murmured. "Question is, how are we going to rescue Aunt Margaret?"

Susan bit her lip. "Poor Aunt Margaret. Alone and scared out of her wits. What *will* we do?"

"We've got to get the sheriff," Danny said firmly. "But we can't leave her here alone either."

"I'll go," Susan said quietly. "Dad probably isn't home yet, but I'll call the sheriff and lead him here to the cave." She swallowed hard. "I just hope he believes such a fantastic story!"

Danny put out a hand. "Before you go, you'd better take a sandwich with you. I don't know about you two, but I'm about to starve. And look, Susan, hurry, will you?"

She nodded her blond head. "I sure will!"

While Danny dug a sandwich from the bag, Scotty shoved the boat out into the stream again and forced it back the way they had come. He paused when the sound of rushing water came to their ears. Far enough!

Susan scrambled out of the tiny boat, almost upsetting it. "Please be careful! Oh and, Scotty, should I bring the sheriff to the tunnel or to the cave?"

"Bring him to the cave," Scotty replied. "And *you're* the one to be careful, Sue. One slip and we've *all* had it!"

"I will," she promised, but her words were lost in the sound of the waterfall. She gave a leap sideways and was gone. Danny and Scotty sat staring at each other blankly.

"Well, where do we go from here?"

Scotty pulled out another sandwich and offered it to Danny. "We had better eat something before we do anything."

Scotty's stomach lurched at the thought of food, but he forced it down anyway. Sorrow over Rocky was still too keen for him to want to eat. Yet there were greater matters at stake now than even Rocky, and he had to be ready to meet them.

"What do you suppose they intend to do with Aunt Margaret?" Danny asked.

"Who knows? I doubt if those men would stop at anything to get that doll."

"And right here on your own ranch, too."

Scotty heaved a sigh. "Well, on the border anyhow. But we're so many miles away from the ranch buildings and being right in the wildest country in these parts, a person could hide out for months and not be discovered. After all, Tracey was here for awhile, and no one ever saw him."

Danny wadded up the piece of waxed paper his sandwich had been wrapped in and laid it carefully outside the boat. "All set?"

"OK," Scotty replied. "Let's go back and see what's happening. I don't know what we could do to help things, but it makes me feel better, just being around."

Danny grinned. "Sure it does, Scot."

Scotty gave his friend an odd look. Then slowly Scotty's words came back to him. He smiled. Yes, it made him feel better to be near Aunt Margaret in this trouble, even if she didn't know that he was there. After all, seeing a lonely old woman in such fearful trouble would touch anyone's heart, wouldn't it?

The boys sat close in the middle of the boat and let it move slowly along as before. Though the temptation to turn on the light in this terrible blackness was great, they agreed it would be better to save the batteries for a real emergency.

There were moments when the fellows felt their skin crawling from fear, and they asked God to protect them and show them what to do when they got to the end of this strange journey. Several times Scotty cried out to his heavenly Father to take care of Aunt Margaret and help her not to be too frightened.

At last a stream of pale light could be seen through a hole twice the size of a basketball. The boys slid out of the boat now and let it go on without them. Standing there in the icy water, they ducked to see through into the cave.

Scotty gritted his teeth in a flash of anger. Aunt Margaret was still sitting as before. Only now she was weeping softly, and there were red welts down one side of her face. Scotty could tell the welts were from a man's hand. In the cave with her was Taggart, a heavy man with a face like a bulldog.

Taggart moved with the ease of a panther, in spite of his weight. "OK, sister," he growled. "It's just you and me now. Looney's taken the horse and gone to Oracle for supplies. He won't be back until after dark. Mr. Karl has gone to the ranch to look for the doll. There's no one there right now, and he'll ransack the place." His eyes narrowed until they were small and beady.

Scotty's heart seemed to stop, and then suddenly it was racing madly. Mr. Karl at the ranch! Susan going there alone! Susan was in the greatest danger of her whole life. And the fellows couldn't do a thing to help. It was too late for that. Then swiftly the boys were faced with the situation before them once more.

Taggart dropped to one knee and picked the doll up from its folds of tissue paper. Angrily, he jerked the string.

> At the end of the river,
> Where you can't get through,
> Just look down;
> There's treasure for you!

Suddenly the man slung the doll across the room and strode back to Aunt Margaret. He shook her savagely, and his face was red with anger. "Where is it? *Tell me where that doll is!*"

Chapter Eleven

DIAMONDS IN THE ROUGH

SCOTTY'S THOUGHTS were racing, and his heart was thundering. He felt torn in four directions. There was sorrow over Rocky, fear for his sister, wonderment over the third message that so clearly said the diamonds were practically in their hands, and terror for Aunt Margaret.

Taggart had stopped shaking Aunt Margaret, but his eyes were burning with hatred. "Where's the doll, old woman?"

Aunt Margaret was sobbing in terror, but she only shook her head. Scotty marveled that she would not tell where the doll was. Her concern for Susan was greater than her concern for herself.

"You'll tell," the man threatened harshly. "I'll find a way to make you tell if it's the last thing I ever do!"

With these words, the man grabbed up his western hat and stalked out of the room. The Coleman lantern swayed awkwardly from above, and the shadows began to dance over the rock walls. Silence, filled only with Aunt Margaret's sobs, swept the scene.

Scotty clamped his jaws tight. "I'm going in. I won't blame you a bit, Danny, if you want to go back the way we came."

Danny appeared to be very busy with something in front of him, and Scotty dared not wait to see what his friend was doing. With only a little trouble Scotty scrambled through the opening in front of him.

Hearing the sound, Aunt Margaret turned her head quickly to see what new event was taking place. She would have cried out for both fear and joy except that Scotty motioned for her to be quiet.

With lightning movements, he grabbed a knife that lay beside a bedroll. Then, whirling over to his aunt, he went to work on the strong, light-weight cords that held her prisoner. He sliced through them swiftly and helped the plump little woman to her feet. She was still crying softly.

"Aunt Margaret, you've got to stop crying," Scotty whispered. "We're going to go down the tunnel, and we mustn't make a sound because we don't know where that guy Taggart is."

Sounds behind him told Scotty that Danny had entered through the small opening and was coming along too. No one spoke as they left the rock chamber and started slowly down the dark tunnel. They had gone but a few paces down the passage when Scotty put out a hand. "Hold it! Your shoes, Aunt Margaret," Scotty whispered. "They make too much noise. Just hold my hand and take it slow and easy."

"Oh, Scotty, I'm so afraid!" the woman whined.

"So are we!" Danny offered softly. "The Lord will take care of us. Just don't panic, whatever you do!"

They longed to use their light and so hurry up this walk through the darkness, but they dared not. It was as still as death, except for the occasional *drip-drip* of water from the ceiling. Then, when a bat dipped low over Aunt Margaret's head, Scotty thought sure the woman was going to faint dead away.

He held her hand tightly. "It's OK. It's just a bat. Aunt Margaret, believe me, Mr. Karl and Taggart are a whole lot worse than a flying bat!" A half smile played about his lips in the blackness. "Aunt Margaret? The Bible says, 'What time I am afraid, I will trust in thee.' Just try trusting the Lord."

Aunt Margaret sniffed softly. "I *don't know* the Lord."

Scotty bit his lip. "You can. You will, too, before you leave the ranch. Come on!"

They inched their way forward. Scotty wondered if Mr. Karl had met his sister and what he had done to her. He wondered if possibly Susan had spotted Mr. Karl first and had gone to Danny's home to call the sheriff. He wondered too how Mr. Karl had made his way to the ranch and how he had kidnapped Aunt Margaret. Well, no time for the answers right now! He did know that these men had a horse in a small enclosure nearby, for he had heard its whinny before—Oh, but no, for Looney had taken the horse and ridden to Oracle. So much for that!

Danny tripped over an unseen rock and threw out a hand to steady himself. All three persons paused breathlessly.

"Who's there?"

Scotty's heart stoood still, and then suddenly it was pounding so hard that he felt weak and dizzy. His hand was like a vise around his aunt's wrist.

Ahead of them was the sound of a man's boots, and a pale light came swinging slowly through the blackness. One of the men was coming back!

Scotty tried to pray but could not. He tried to think, but his mind was blank. There was another room off this tunnel. Where was it? Oh, why couldn't he remember where it was?

Then, through the darkness, was Danny's hand Scotty followed his friend blindly, and all the time he realized that Aunt Margaret was shaking like the pepper tree in their front yard when the wind blew through the branches. Aunt Margare couldn't panic now! She had to hang on a little longer!

The trio passed from the narrow rock tunnel into another chamber, smaller than the one where the men were hiding out. Scotty pulled his frightened aunt back against the wall, watching as great shadows were flung over the walls from the approaching light. It paused momentarily in the rough doorway, then passed on out of sight.

Scotty was breathing a little easier, but Aunt Margaret was trembling from head to foot. Once she slumped a little as if she were fainting, and Scotty cried out desperately for the Lord to uphold her.

"This place is making me feel so creepy that I'm beginning to hear—" Taggart's words, down the corridor, suddenly broke off in amazement and dread. "The old lady's gone!"

Scotty pulled his aunt into the passageway once more. "Come on, Aunt Margaret, if you ever ran, you'd better run now!"

Danny darted ahead of them, shining the light so that all three could see. They were pretty sure that Taggart was still searching the other room and trying to figure out where the woman had disappeared to, so they had a little time. But in another minute or two he'd be hot on their trail, and there was not a second to lose!

"I've got the diamonds," Danny gasped. "If we get away now, we've got it made!"

Scotty thought he was hearing things, but there was no time now to ponder even that.

Suddenly, without a warning of any kind, the brush that covered the opening was taken away and a shadow fell into the tunnel. Mr. Karl was back! And behind them, coming pell-mell, was Taggart!

Chapter Twelve

MR. KARL TRAPS HIMSELF

SCOTTY CAUGHT HIS BREATH. His dark head flung about to see how near Taggart was, and he was alarmed to see the light swaying steadily forward.

Danny had shut off their own flashlight, plunging them into deep shadow. Danny's slim body was flat against the wall, arms thrown out at his sides. Terror raced through his heart.

Ahead of the fellows and coming slowly through the opening was Mr. Karl. Now he paused to pull the brush halfway into the opening, thus hiding it from the outside. Then he started forward.

A lump rose to Scotty's throat and he felt sick. It couldn't happen. Somehow God wouldn't let it happen!

"Karl!" Taggart yelled harshly. "The old lady's gone!"

"What?" Mr. Karl stopped dead still. "What do you mean?"

"The old lady! She's disappeared! Take a look for yourself!"

The trio flattened their bodies against the wall.

Scotty's jaw dropped when he saw a doll hanging limply in the man's hands. He'd been to the ranch. He'd found the doll. *Where was Susan?* The doll didn't worry him, for Scotty knew that the voice box was gone. Apparently Mr. Karl didn't know that just yet.

Here he came in a run. "How could the old woman get away?" he raged. "You blundering idiot, what have you done?"

So far the two men were too excited to see the three shadows. Mr. Karl was looking straight ahead at the dim light. He passed by Danny. Then Aunt Margaret. Suddenly he glimpsed the trio out of the corner of his eye and turned his head, shocked and bewildered. In that moment Scotty, being the last one Mr. Karl would have to pass, thrust out a foot that sent the man sprawling headlong.

"Now!" Scotty yelled. "Come on, Aunt Margaret, as fast as you can!"

It took a few seconds for Mr. Karl to recover himself. Even then he sat for a moment nursing acute pain in the cap of one knee. Taggart was rushing forward, cursing and angry.

There was the sound of a gun shot, then the angry words. "You fool! Wait till I get out of the way!"

The bullet smacked against the tunnel wall beside Scotty and sent dirt and bits of rock trickling

down. Near the opening now, the three people
bolted through brush and all and dropped to the
ground. Other bullets came singing out above
them, and the sounds filled the tunnel with a roar.

"Where to, Scot?" Danny cried. "They'll find us
before you know it!"

Scotty's gaze swept the area. Over to his left
was the small barbed enclosure covered with more
brush where the brown horse was kept. But that
didn't offer any protection. Dear God, what should
they do now?

The voices of the angry men could be heard now
from within the tunnel. A couple more shots
pierced the stillness of these rugged hills. Then
the sound of a terrible roar filled everything!

Jerking his head about, Scotty saw a strange
sight. The earth that covered the tunnel was *caving in!* The vibration of sound had started the dirt
and loose rocks to falling. The men were prisoners.
Or even worse, they might be dead.

Scotty felt a shudder go through him. "Looney's
still around somewhere. Let's get out of here!"

"We can't walk all the way back to the ranch,"
Danny protested weakly. "*We* might make it, but
Aunt Ma—that is, your aunt could never walk that
far."

Aunt Margaret, for once, was silent. In any
other situation, Scotty was sure he'd have burst
out laughing. Her face was smudged with dirt,

her hair was wild, her eyes were popping, and
there was no "dear boys" coming from her lips.
But he felt sorry for her too, for she had been
through a real nightmare, and she was tired and
frightened.

"We'll have to start walking," Scotty said firmly.
"Aunt Margaret, how did Mr. Karl ever manage
to get you here anyway?"

She tried to speak, but her lips were trembling.
"I-I went d-down after the m-mail, and this j-jeep
stopped beside m-me. It was that awful m-man,
Mr. K-Karl. He made me write th-the note and
get in with him." As she talked her nerves seemed
to calm a bit so that she could speak more freely.
Neither was she looking back over her shoulder
any longer. But she was without shoes and so the
boys let her pause to rest.

"The jeep belonged to the ranch where that awful Looney worked. He quit work yesterday. They
tried to make me tell about that doll. But I
wouldn't tell them who I gave it to, though I can-
not understand why a doll could be so important
to three big strong men!"

"Didn't you hear the message that was in the
doll there in the tunnel?"

Her eyes asked an unspoken question. "Yes, but
it didn't make any sense to me."

"It didn't make any sense to them either, Aunt

Margaret, without the first doll, the one the toy store sold to you by mistake."

Danny pulled a small bag from the pocket of his jeans. "But the three messages together made a whole lot of sense. While you went on in with your aunt, Scotty, I discovered a shelf there by that little opening. Look what was on that shelf!"

Triumphantly opening the little bag, Danny produced several pebble-like stones. They were clear and beautiful even though uncut as yet.

"Wow!" Scotty breathed softly.

Aunt Margaret touched one of the uncut stones. "How lovely! Why, I do believe they might be first quality. They're the ones that are free from all imperfections. My husband was a lapidary, you know!" Aunt Margaret was twittering again, but it didn't bother Scotty as much as before. He was too thankful that she was alive and still in Arizona.

"Yes, yes," Aunt Margaret went on. "A diamond is the hardest material known to man, but my husband was one of the best stonecutters ever. And these! When they're finished they'll be the most beautiful stones imaginable." Suddenly Aunt Margaret broke off, and tears slid down her cheeks.

"Aunt Margaret, what's the matter?"

"I was so scared," she cried. "It was just awful in that cave! And now those men are there in that cave, and who knows how badly hurt they are?"

So her nerves were shaken worse than Scotty had suspected.

"And you, Scotty," the woman went on, sobbing quietly, the tears making muddy little rivers down her face. "Your beautiful horse is dead because of me. And yet you came and saved me from those men! I'm a terrible, mean old woman. Please forgive me."

Scotty felt miserable. "You're the one who has to forgive me, Aunt Margaret. I don't know what was the matter with me, but I'm sorry, honest I am. You didn't mean to leave the corral open, and I acted just terrible."

He stood straight, looking out across the canyons that sprawled out at his feet. Suddenly he felt good. His heart was clean and he felt like he'd grown a couple of inches spiritually. But now there was work to be done. Susan had to be found, and the men in the tunnel, criminals or not, needed help. Looney had to be caught and—

"Someone's coming," Danny whispered.

Scotty dropped down out of sight. "Looney?"

"I don't know!"

They waited, half concealed by a low-growing pine tree, as a horse came slowly into view.

Chapter Thirteen

UNFOLDING OF A MIRACLE

BEHIND THE BAY HORSE coming slowly up over the rocks was another horse. And yet another. And behind this one was a black horse, upon which sat *Susan!*

"Susan!" The glad cry escaped Scotty's lips almost before he intended, and a moment later he was dashing breathlessly toward the sheriff and his men. For indeed it was the sheriff who sat upon the leading horse.

"Scotty!" Susan slid from the saddle. Her keen blue eyes took in Danny, who was grinning broadly, and Aunt Margaret, who was giving away once more to tears. "Aunt Margaret! Oh, Scot, how did you ever do it?"

"It's too long to tell now, Susan. The main thing is that Aunt Margaret is safe." Scotty swiftly turned his attention to the sheriff. "Sir, the men—two of them—are buried up there in the tunnel. They were shooting at us, when all of a sudden the tunnel just began caving in."

The sheriff's eyes narrowed. "Are you sure about this, son?"

"Oh, yes sir, I'm sure all right! Taggart and Mr. Karl are their names, and they're the ones who've been causing all the trouble about the dolls and all." Scotty broke off here, for he didn't know how much Susan had told the sheriff, and he didn't want to go breaking the story over the man in pieces. It made little enough sense the way it was.

The sheriff turned in the saddle and spoke to one of his men. "Go back to the ranch, Craig, and call in for a rescue party. Wait until the men arrive, and then get them here as fast as possible."

The faraway whinny of a horse sounded as the sheriff and his deputies went on to the cave. Scotty and Susan were ordered back with Aunt Margaret now, and the woman was put on Susan's horse. Since Aunt Margaret was *not* a rider, Scotty took the reins in his hand and led the horse down the slope.

The neigh of the horse sounded again and Scotty turned with a puzzled look on his face.

Susan explained, "It's probably the horse Mr. Karl was riding. I caught a glimpse of it *and* Mr. Karl, for they were just coming back as I got near the ranch. I saw that big black and white horse, and it nearly scared me out of my wits. Mr. Karl must have been watching the ranch from here with binoculars, and he knew everyone was gone. Oh, and he *did* get the doll."

Scotty chuckled. "The men will die when they find out the treasure was within easy reach all the time!"

Danny snapped his fingers in sudden remembrance. "I forgot to give the diamonds to the sheriff." He lifted his eyebrows. "And, as long as I'm remembering things, why are we walking? We left our horses up there, remember?"

"Yes, but I took them to the ranch with me when I went," Susan said quickly. "I was afraid one of the men might see them and wonder."

It was dusk when the trio leading the horse arrived back at the Diamond W Ranch. Mr. Hanson was there, looking bewildered and a little frightened. Scotty's mother had been home for two hours. She was waiting for them to come back and her forehead was knotted into a frown. So much had happened that Scotty's parents knew nothing about yet.

Aunt Margaret took a hot bath and was put to bed with a sedative. Scotty, Susan, and Danny dropped down in the living room and unfolded the story as they had lived it and wondered about the parts as yet untold.

It was 10:30 that night when the sheriff and the rescue party arrived back at the ranch with two bedraggled looking men in tow. Mr. Karl and

Taggart were finished, and one look at their faces
said they knew it all too well. At almost the same
moment a deputy stopped to check with the sheriff. A tall, lanky, sullen-eyed Looney stood beside
him.

"He was sneaking back to the cave, sir. He'd
been to Oracle for supplies, and the storekeeper
tipped me off that he was acting strangely and
might bear investigation. I think he's one of them."

"He sure is!" Danny cried. "And so is the owner
of that toy store who had the dolls for them."

Things were squared away by the sheriff as he
ordered all three men taken into custody. Then,
after everyone was gone from the ranch but him,
he gathered the Hanson family and Danny together for a last pow-wow.

"It was a pretty slick operation." He sighed
heavily, accepted the coffee Mrs. Hanson brought
in, and began to speak slowly. "It seems that the
jewel robbery took place in New York some months
back by the three we just took into custody. Things
were too hot for them, and they couldn't decide
on a hiding place because they didn't trust one
another. They were afraid that, while they were
separated, one of them would sneak back and
steal the diamonds. Tracey was Mr. Karl's brother
and was wanted by the law at that time, and it
seems that all three men trusted Tracey. So the
diamonds were given to him, and he hid out here

on the ranch in that lonely, isolated cave for nearly a whole summer. Of course you already know that he hid the diamonds there, practically inside the cave. Then, after he went back to his job at the doll factory, he made these three special talking boxes and dressed the dolls for their special job. Naturally, he did all this on his own away from the factory, but he used the needed materials from work. Tracey was killed, and then the first doll disappeared and— Well, you know the story from there."

Mr. Hanson shook his head slowly. "What a story! And to think of what these kids must have gone through."

"And poor Margaret," Scotty's mother said. "She must have been terrified! Thank God, the children took matters into their own hands in just the way they did."

Sleep came quickly for the boys that night, despite the fact that they were back in the guest-house. The day had been long and rugged. They had showered, eaten, and tumbled into bed. Neither of them could remember too clearly the moment his head had touched the pillows!

When the pale streaks of dawn began tracing their fingers through the sky, however, Scotty's dark eyes opened slowly. For long moments he lay staring at the ceiling, his fingers locked together under his head. What had been the purpose in all

this? For him, that is? Why had Aunt Margaret
been in the picture? Why had Scotty felt as he
had toward her—felt so deeply that he'd nearly
backslidden? Why had Rocky been killed? Why
so many things?

Very quietly Scotty crawled out of bed, stepped
into his slippers, draped his robe about his shoulders, and left the guesthouse. His gaze was drawn
toward the corral. How empty it seemed without
his great white horse nickering softly for him.

Without meaning to or wanting to, Scotty's
steps turned in that direction. Softly he opened
the corral gate and slipped inside. The smell of
hay and of horses came sharply to his nostrils, but
it was a smell he'd grown up with, a smell he
loved!

Rocky!

A sob rose from deep within Scotty's chest, but
he held it back. Oh, it was lonely without the
beautiful horse. It was so hard to understand and
believe that the thunder of his hoofs would never
again echo through the ranch, that his whinny
would never again welcome his master's touch.

Turning, Scotty headed for the tack room where
the saddles and brushes were kept. There on the
narrow shelf lay the New Testament. It was covered by a heavy layer of dust which Scotty first
blew and then wiped carefully away.

It was still very early, and no one was stirring

about yet. Even his father was sleeping later than usual. Only the desert creatures were up and hurrying about busily in these early hours. A cottontail nibbled at a bit of grass, perhaps preparing a nest for a new litter of rabbits. Two does were climbing the game trail high in the hills, getting ready to bed down for the day. And the funny little gophers, always a delight to watch, were scampering to and from their holes, as though their work were more important than the work of any other living creature. Or maybe they were simply playing a game of follow-the-leader.

In the quiet Scotty took the New Testament and went to sit on a bale of hay. He opened the book and began to read. Then his eyes blurred strangely, and he had to lay the book aside. For the words he had read were: "My son, despise not thou the chastening of the Lord, nor faint when thou art rebuked of him: For whom the Lord loveth he chasteneth." God was saying, *You're my son, Scotty, but I've had to correct and discipline you so that your life would shine more clearly for me. Don't you see that it's only because I love you?*

Yes, God had been perfecting him. God wanted him to be *first quality*, like those diamonds. And the human heart, like the diamonds, was very hard. The heavenly Father surely was the master Stonecutter, and He knew just where to strike the precious stone, just how to shape and to polish, to make it perfect.

Slowly Scotty began to see himself as a diamond in the rough, a diamond in which God saw something very worthwhile. He was shaping Scotty's life in a way to make it the finest for His sake. Realizing this, it was easier for him to accept many of the things that had been ruffling his feathers.

After placing this day into God's hands Scotty replaced the New Testament. The faraway sound of a whinny came to his ears, accompanied in a moment by the sound of galloping hoofs. Scotty lifted his head and his nostrils flared wide. There was the sound of thunder in those hoofs!

He closed his eyes and shook his head fiercely. No, no, no! It couldn't— What a beautiful, powerful-looking horse that was, galloping toward the corral. A black and white— Oh, oh! That was the horse Mr. Karl had been riding. But why was he heading for the Diamond W corral? There were long red ribbons of blood on the horse's belly. That meant that the animal had jumped the little barbed enclosure. Now why would a horse do a crazy thing like that? Surely there had been food and water for—

Those eyes! The long powerful legs, the silken mane and flowing tail! Why, the horse was nipping Scotty's ear. A soft whinny filled the air, and Mr. Hanson stepped out the kitchen door to see

Aunt Margaret was emerging from the bedroom door and walking toward the corral.

Scotty swallowed through a dry throat, hardly daring to think, to hope. Rocky was dead. His mother and Susan had seen him! He was battered beyond recognition. Beyond— Then how could they have been sure?

As in a dream, Scotty lifted a hand and rubbed it over one of the black spots on the horse's back. Mr. Hanson was there by now, rubbing a hard hand along the animal's flanks in bewilderment. Then he lifted his head and smiled.

"He bears the brand of the Diamond W, son."

Scotty's eyes were suddenly very shiny. "Rocky? Dad? This—*this is Rocky!*"

"It certainly is! That horse that was killed must have been the old stallion that led the band of wild horses." Still the man explored this strange horse. "Scotty? Mr. Karl must have needed another horse for a little while. He'd probably seen Rocky through binoculars and liked him. So he stole him during the night, then painted black spots on him. He figured Rocky wouldn't be seen, and he didn't need him for very long. He only rode him near the ranch when he was sure no one was here. Son, God has given you a miracle!"

Aunt Margaret, draping her plump body over the corral fence, suddenly began to cry. "Oh, I'm so thankful I wasn't at fault. I'm so glad your horse is alive, Scotty."

A slow smile curved Scotty's lips. He could hardly take it all in. Rocky was alive and well and nipping at his ear just like always. The boy reached up to swing his arms about that powerful neck. Mr. Hanson had gone to get some salve for the horse's cuts.

"God only gave him back to me, Aunt Margaret, after He'd showed me some other things first. And one of them was that He is able to fill the emptiness from any loss." His heart added sincerely, *Lord Jesus, what a wonderful Saviour You are! And how much I love You!*

There was a wistful look in Aunt Margaret's eyes. Yes, Scotty was sure she would find Christ too before leaving the ranch.

Butch, just arriving on the scene, sat thumping his stub of a tail eagerly, looking pretty pleased about the outcome of everything.

"Scotty, I can't tell you how glad I am. Oh, you dear boy, you do deserve the very best. The way you risked your life for me yesterday and—!"

Aunt Margaret was beginning to twitter again. Scotty lifted his dark eyes from his beloved horse and smiled at her.